# Antônio Torres

# The Land

translated by Margaret A. Neves

readers international

The title of this book in Portuguese is *Essa Terra*, first published in São Paulo by Editora/Atica S.A. in 1976 and now in its seventh edition.

Cover and internal illustrations by Brazilian artist Djanira
Design by Jan Brychta
Typeset by Grassroots Typeset, London NW6
Printed and bound in Great Britain by Richard Clay
(The Chaucer Press) Ltd., Bungay, Suffolk


ISBN 0-930523-24-5 Hardcover
ISBN 0-930523-25-3 Paperback

"No battle is ever won...They are not even fought. The field only reveals to man his own folly and despair, and victory is an illusion of philosophers and fools."
William Faulkner, *The Sound and the Fury*

# From the author to his dead cousin

Dear José Giése da Cruz,

It was in Junqueiro da Bahia (in 1970, I think) that I told you of a story I was writing about Junco, and which started like this:

It doesn't matter where this place is. It is very far away from you, because Junco barely appears on the map....

That was our last meeting, but I did not know it at the time. We talked a lot in that month, do you remember? You told me many things as we travelled around Junco, going on to Nova Soure, Pombal and Jorro, visiting our relatives. You wanted to help me with the story, I knew; but you weren't able to wait. That's life.

I remember stopping in Mimoso. We got to talking with the old farmers about the square in Junco, which was going to be paved. You asked them:

Does the mayor show you how to plant beans? Has he taught you to choose seed? Does he know fertilizers? No? Then he's not a good mayor.

Dear Giése, this is not your story, although it has much to do with you and me, with the late Lela de Tote and with Humberto Vieira. You remember: after many comings and goings to and from São Paulo, Lela went down for the count, left this world for a better one, as the saying goes. You followed his example, leaving behind great sadness and so many unanswered questions. But Humberto and I are still here and we still think life is worth living.

You share this story with Sonia and Gabriel, my wife and son whom, unfortunately, you will never meet. You share it with dear Durvalice and Irineu, my parents, and with my ten brothers and sisters whom you helped so much, helping me to get through high school in Alagoinhas, Bahia.

Can you hear me, for God's sake?

Your cousin,
Antônio

# PART ONE

## The Land Calls Me

# I

"IF HE'S ALIVE he'll come back someday, I always said."

"What did you say?"

At that hour I could draw a straight line from the top of my head to the sun and climb up it, just like a monkey on a rope, until I reached heaven—I never needed to know the time.

It was noon, and I knew because I was stepping on a shadow the size of my hat, the only sign of life in the familiar old square where no one poked his head outside for fear of roasting his brains. The only ones crazy enough to be there were myself and the old man mounted on a sweating horse, who had turned up like a ghost inside a cloud of dust to delay me beneath the Lord's cauldron.

"Anybody in these parts will swear to it, anybody with a memory under his hat and decency in his heart. I always said he'd come back some day. And hasn't he?"

"You're right."

"Changed much? I hope at least he hasn't forgotten the way to my house. We're of the same blood."

"He hasn't forgotten, Uncle," I answered, feeling that I was making a necessary clarification not just to one man, but to an entire population for whom my brother's return seemed to have greater significance even than the time Dr.

Dantas Junior came to announce that our town had been put on the map, thanks to his word and his efforts as our well-chosen Federal Representative. It was a most wonderful day, as wonderful as an election day (though without the tumult, the beer and the food of election days) because everything happened suddenly, without warning. The representative got up on a hastily made podium in front of the market, waved his dusty jacket over his head and said that the loyal and hospitable Junco was now a proper town. Now we could manage our own affairs without having to answer to the municipality of Inhambupe—and it was precisely that part of his speech people liked best. Still, even that day is fading from memory, though nothing else has happened since.

What really hadn't changed at all was the place: mud-brick houses with red tile roofs and lime whitewash. But the burning question was to know if my brother still remembered each and every relative he had left behind in these parts, each one: he who, without having a square inch of land where he could fall down dead, one day hitched a ride in a truck and disappeared into the great world to be transformed as if by enchantment into a rich handsome man with gold teeth, a loose, hot, wool suit, Ray-Ban sunglasses, a transistor radio (talkative little bastard) and a watch that sparkled brighter than the sunlight. A monument in flesh and blood. Living proof that this place could sire great men—and I, not even born when he went away, was on my way to see if I could rouse the great man out of two decades of sleep, because the great man seemed to come back only to stay in bed. Get up, you old dog, before the bats eat you. Wake up, before the suffering soul of your beloved grandfather asks you for a complete account of your travels. Hurry, because he's coming out of his grave to tap you on the shoulder: "Seventy of them. You're worth seventy of these fellows from here." "Why, Padrinho?" "Because you've already been to four states, haven't you, boy?"

I was dying to go for a swim in the old pond (yes, the one we'll all drown in) and wanted my brother to go with me. I was thinking of finding a jenny-ass, the most spirited one around, for the famous Nelo to recapture the ecstasies of an old love.

"Tell him he was born right there," my uncle pointed toward the slaughter-pen. "And tell him I carried him on my shoulders."

"Nelo remembers everything and everyone, Uncle. I've never seen such a fine memory," I insisted, so as not to leave the slightest doubt in his mind. Only then would he allow me to continue on my way.

"I'm pleased," my uncle smiled, adopting his formal, serious manner; and the horse covered me with another cloud of dust.

My sandal crushed my shadow as I advanced through a silent, suspended moment, as if there were no wind left in the world. An omen, perhaps? Something horrible, most horrible, might be happening.

"Nelo!" I yelled from the street. "Come and teach me how to float on top of a *mulungu* trunk. They tell me you used to be good at it!" I didn't hear what he answered, rather, there was no answer. There wasn't, yet there was. Out on the farm I once heard about a ghostly bird that would come to bother a young girl every time she went out into the yard at night, at any hour. Perhaps my brother had just chirped into my ear through the beak of that unseen

3

night-bird in which I had never believed. Shaken, I ran up and knocked on the door, and one knock was enough to push it open, so that I was the first to see him hanging from a rope fastened to the hammock hook.

"Stop that, Nelo!" I slapped him on the left side of his face, and it must have been a hard slap, because his head turned and fell toward the right. "Stop it, for the love of God!" I repeated, slapping his other cheek, and again his head rolled to the opposite side.

There.

I would never again want to climb a rope up to heaven.

## II

So it was that a place forgotten in time awoke from its stupor to make the sign of the cross. Junco: a scarlet bird called Sofrê, which learned to sing the national anthem. A speckled hen called Sophie, which learned to hide her nests. An ox named Sufferer. A yoke: winter begins, summer ends. The most beautiful sunrise in the world and the longest sunset. The smell of rosemary and the words lily-of-the-valley. I never saw a lily-of-the-valley. Shards: of red tile, of glass. The sound of hoes being sharpened, of cattle-drivers' mournful calls along the road, of men scratching a living from the land. My mother's black tobacco-juice spittle, my father's mute complaints, my grandmother's red and white roses. Roses of love: "I'll love you till I die."

This is the land that spawned me.

"Lampião the bandit passed through here."

"No he didn't. He sent a message saying he was

4

coming but he didn't actually come."

"Why not?"

"Why should Lampião waste his time coming here? This is the end of the world."

Girls looking out the window at the road seem to say—yes, it is the end of the world. They are dreaming of the boys who went to São Paulo and never came back to fetch them. They are waiting for the bank clerks from Alagoinhas and the oil workers from Petrobrás. They are waiting, but not for country hicks. City boys only. "They'll eat their words some day, they'll die man-crazy old maids with shrivelled cunts," growl the frustrated bachelors. Horny is a dirty word and comes from the devil. Like sin, like other dirty words: cunt, asshole, son-of-a-bitch. Cows, heifers, mares and jennies also have cunts. They're not so choosey.

"Even the married ones have lost their heads, dragging their men and their daughters off to the big towns." This refrain is heard at Pedro Infante's general store and bar, sanctuary for complainers. "Many's the husband who goes go off in search of work, only to come back alone and penniless. The place for a farmer is on the farm."

Slow and solitary, Junco survives its griefs in the knowledge that it has seen worse times, and still bears witness to past disasters. In 1932 the place was almost crossed off the map of the State of Bahia and inscribed on the map of hell, during the worst drought the region had ever known, a drought marked to this day in each cattle skull impaled on a fence post, to bring good luck.

"People fell down dead from hunger and thirst, just like the cattle. It cut you to the heart to see it."

The first rains of '33 promised an abundant harvest,

but they didn't go beyond the promise. Later came deluge, ague and malaria: and the people died trembling with cold. "It's worse in wartime, when the son cries out and the father can't hear him," says Caetano Jabá. He wasn't the only one to follow the rebel uprising of Antônio Conselheiro, although he had been the only one to come back alive, telling the story of the soldier whose throat he had cut with his tobacco-knife as the soldier peacefully ate a plateful of *jabá*-bird meat and dry manioc flour on the bank of a stream. Instead of a medal, they gave Caetano a nickname and a hoe with which he digs his sustenance to this day, at the age of a hundred-odd.

"In the year two thousand this old world will be burned up by a ball of fire, and after that Judgement Day will come," says Jabá, teaching the Sacred Prophecies as he rests from the burden of death-guilt he carries on his shoulders. "And I know that day isn't far off. Why just look here: our grandfathers had plenty of pasture, our fathers had much less and we don't have any." The other men listen attentively to Caetano Jabá—he has lived and experienced much. "That's in the Holy Scriptures too. Much land, few signs. Many heads, few hats. One flock for one shepherd."

"Here come the hicks from Junco," say the people in Inhambupe.

Or used to say, when the open-bed truck carrying the yearly load of people to Our Lady of Candeias stopped at the gas pump outside the Hotel Rex. The people would sit on hard wooden benches under a canvas tarpaulin. Now the road bypasses the town, and Inhambupe has nobody to insult.

Let us pray for the soul of the departed Antônio

Conselheiro. Much do we owe him. When he was in Inhambupe he was stoned without mercy. He called down a curse:

"May this place grow just like the tail of a jackass!"

The people asked themselves, "How does a jackass' tail grow?"

"Downwards."

"But all tails grow downwards."

"But when the jackass' tail grows, the owner cuts it to make the animal more valuable."

The asphalt road to Paulo Afonso didn't get this far, but then, it left Inhambupe on one side too. The place grows like a jackass' tail.

All that remains is the waiting, under the open sky.

"Any day now the Antichrist will appear. That'll be the first sign. Then the sun will grow, and turn into a ball the size of an oxcart wheel, and then—" Papa used to say, Mama used to say, everyone used to say.

Nobody said, however, whether the coming of Ancar was in the Holy Scriptures. Ancar: the bank that arrived in a jeep one Sunday morning at Mass time, to lend money to whoever had a few acres of land. The men in the jeep went straight to the church and asked the priest to announce who they were during the sermon. The priest agreed. He spoke of progress, of the benefits for all. The bank had the President's guarantee.

"If the President guarantees it, it must be a good thing," the first to say a word in favor of the newcomers was facing them in the doorway of the general store. But he wilted when he heard the unexpected advice:

"Plant sisal. It's making lots of money."

Nobody knew how to plant sisal, that was the problem.

The men from the bank discussed, explained, promised machines, money and every possible help.

Later the jeep came back, bringing the expired promissory notes. Only then—and for the first time in their lives—did the men of Junco begin to comprehend that a priest could be mistaken.

The day he saw the men with the jeep Nelo decided to leave. He was seventeen years old. He would still take three more years to tear himself loose from Papa's trouserleg, three years dreaming every night about the clothes and talk of those bank employees...the clothes and talk of men who, without a doubt, had very good luck with women.

# III

Twenty years ahead, twenty years behind. And me in the middle, like two hands of a clock forever stopped, marking always the halfway point of something—like an old pendulum clock that long ago lost the rhythm and direction of the hours. That's how I feel, and not only now that I know how everything ended.

I am in front of him, at the door of the lodging house called a hotel by its owner, an outsider. The owner doesn't know him. He insists that he come in and inspect the rooms, the bath facilities and the general cleanliness of everything. He turns on the taps to show the color of the water, strained many times before passing from the barrels into the tank. Limpid and clear, like the picture on the television that flickers from six in the morning to ten at night, at least on nights when the generator isn't broken. The pharmacist told me who the man approaching the hotel was: many people didn't recognize him. I arrive, interrupting the well-worn and sincere conversation of the hotel manager. The smile of the newly-arrived guest is also sincere as he shakes my hand. "A pleasure," he says. Manners from other places, I think, shaking my head from side to side in astonishment. I almost answer, "Thank you very much," like men from the farmlands when greeted by a stranger. It was an unexpected meeting, as strange a meeting between two brothers as could be. At that moment I didn't yet know I had just crossed the bridge that would bring me to the end of an era.

It's true, we never knew each other personally; hence all my difficulty. I was only aware of feeling rather foolish, without knowing what to say besides "come in." "A pleasure"—was that the sum of everything? Only two words to appease twenty years of longing? Uncertain, fumbling, my hand jerks forward to offer itself, advancing to grasp the handle of his suitcase. My palm still felt the cold sweat of his. Cold hands, warm heart, I even remember thinking, asking myself if he was exactly the way I had imagined him, if I had a clean pair of sheets and a blanket, enough bread for supper tonight, food for lunch tomorrow, and why didn't you let us know you were coming, how long do you plan to stay?—the type of thing we don't say to relatives so they won't think they're unwelcome. The truth was, I was in no position to put him up. Yet even so I was saying:

"There's no reason for you to spend money on a hotel."

"I didn't know I had a brother here." He removes my hand from the suitcase and adds, "That's all right. I'll take it myself."

The suitcase made me think of the post office and the fat monthly envelopes of earlier times. Real live money from São Paulo. I remembered my mother, too: "I wish I had one more son like him. Just one more would be enough."

Nelo, Nelo, Nelo.

A lullaby, a tune, a song.

Nelo, Nelo, Nelo.

We imagine him silhouetted against the setting sun as it goes down behind the mountain, disappearing over the edge of the world.

Nelo, Nelo, Nelo.

São Paulo is there behind the mountain, follow your brother's example.

Nelo, Nelo, Nelo.

There were twelve of us, including a sister who died; but he was the only one who mattered.

Nelo, Nelo, Nelo. "Just one more would be enough."

Our shade at noonday, our daily bread.

"Look who's here!"

Come in, make yourself at home.

What a pleasure!


"First son, first grandson,"—maybe that's what he is thinking as he makes a complete tour of the house, room by room, corner by corner. Now he is in the kitchen, sitting on the old wood-burning stove, looking uncomprehendingly at the gas stove I use, which served to boil the last pots of tea my grandmother drank. Eighteen children and their respective spouses fight over the house contents while the estate is being settled. I live here alone because it's free. With the money I make in the Mayor's office, I can only live in rent-free lodging. I once lived in Feira de Santana,

I went to high school there, but things didn't work out.

He gets up and stands in the doorway to the back yard. He complains that the flowers are dying. If my grandmother were alive she would have looked after them. He asks about Papa.

"He sold the farm with the farmhouse and the house in town, paid his debts, drank up the change, and then moved to Feira de Santana."

Didn't he know that? Of course he did.

"Poor old man," he says, and asks about Mama.

"She went ahead of us, to enrol us at school. The old man stayed here, not knowing what to do with himself, miserable, cursing his luck. From time to time he would go to Feira. But he got tired of going back and forth; he started drinking and quarrelling with everybody. One day he went off down the road in a truck, singing to himself."

"Poor old man," he says again and asks about the kids.

"Three of them are in Feira: the younger ones. The others are spread out—" here I open my arms from North to South. "You'll have to travel around a lot if you want to see them, every one. But you won't have to go farther than Salvador."

"I feel really sorry for Papa." His voice was still the same as when he said, "Poor old man." He seemed worried, and his worry grew as he asked, "The money I send, is it enough?"

I believe that was the only time we looked each other in the eye during all the days we spent together. Four blessed weeks that stretched out like eternity. Anyone who doubts can try it: if you ever have a brother to stay, and don't know what to do with him, you'll find out.

"I wish it was," I say.

"And Papa, doesn't he help out at all?"

I didn't answer him, just shook my head—and it was then that the idea of the motionless hands of a clock occurred to me. I bit my lips, aware of what I was doing and feeling; I could no longer hide my bitterness. I suppose my own bitter face was the best explanation for everything. I didn't need a mirror to know how I looked to Nelo. I wanted to say: tell me about good things, about all the fine adventures you've had, give me something to dream of. But he insisted, questioning again and again as he cracked his knuckles nervously, making me nervous too.

"What about the others? Don't they help out either?"

It was as if he were saying, Am I going to spend my life supporting them?

My answer was yes. Yes, Nelo old man, the others hardly manage to eat, and as for me, I drew a cross on the wall and vowed by it that that madhouse would never see another penny of mine, even if I had money to burn. They could all die in need before my eyes and I wouldn't even bother to see they were buried. Because of all they did to me, my whole life, mainly what they did to me during the years when I needed them, on account of a school course. The others feel the same way, I'm sure of it. Only one star shone among us. Pay for that, preferably in gold. Everything is fixed in my memory. Listen:

"Nobody does anything for me. Nobody helps me with anything."

Do you recognise that voice? Listen some more. Listen:

"Twelve children, but I feel so alone. If it weren't for Nelo…"

Wait, there's more.

"I'm not going to iron your clothes. I'm not your maid."

And now, pay attention:

"Anybody who doesn't like it can leave."

So I left. Want some advice? Go and live with them for a while. Then you won't need my explanations. Try to understand what it's like to spend your life inside a bagful of cats with a hole in the bottom. The cats go in, scratch each other and work their way down to the bottom of the bag. I put up with it as long as I could. Now...

There wasn't time to think or say anything more. The house was filling up with people and suddenly he was all smiles, making me ask myself what kind of man this was who could pass from sadness to happiness with a simple hug-and-handshake. I won't deny it: I experienced a strange sort of pleasure at that little-lost-lamb expression on his face every time one of my answers pricked him.

"Don't forget, it was me who persuaded your father to let you go away,"—the first visitor had come to collect the long-term interest on his loan.

"Papa wouldn't even discuss the subject," chuckled figures from the past.

"And what kind of homecoming is this, without even a celebration?" A festive voice demands fireworks, confetti, music.

"Stand us a drink! I want to see the color of São Paulo money." Daring relatives glance about in search of his suitcase.

"Not even a little souvenir for your cousins? Don't tell me you forgot about me!"

My aunt. Good grief, she's already heard.

"This one here is going to be just like you. He's smart as the devil." She raps the head of the boy who is smart as the devil. "Now there's a son for you!" (not hers, naturally). How many years have you been sending money to your mother, Nelo?"

"Can I keep track?" Saying this, he appears very different from a few minutes before. He seems to take pride in his role of faithful son.

"Ah, Nelo, you're filthy rich, aren't you?"

"I get along," he says, but his words do nothing to destroy our illusions.

"A lucky boy. He was always lucky, ever since he was a kid."

An aunt of this aunt arrives, one we are all obliged to address as Aunt, kiss her hand and ask her blessing, even if we meet her ten times in the same day.

"Boy, are you the one who lives soooooo far away?"

Roads that lead away but not back, disappearing into the farthest reaches of the imagination, in that voice spinning out league upon league.

"Yes, I'm the one, Aunt," he says, almost overcome with joy.

"Boy, come closer, over heeeeere." Now her voice reels the road in, shrinking it, bringing the distances towards her, near her, inside her heart.

"Today everything has to come to a halt in this town, Nelo old man," speaks the festive voice, and other voices join it in a chorus announcing the news: finally, an evening with something to talk about.

And they all go off, like a herd of animals heading to the waterhole for a drink.

I go after them—drawn, pulled, following the herd.

"Congratulations, congratulations!" they repeat again and again, as if I had won a fortune in the lottery.

# IV

"Another of the damned has gone to Hell," preaches mad Alcino, at the church door.

People say Alcino went mad because of his vices. But this time nobody bothers to see if he has hair on the palms of his sinful hands. Everyone knows that the crazy man is speaking the truth, for a person who kills himself is truly damned

"The Devil knots the rope, and God refuses to cut it. God doesn't help a man with no religion. Look at yourselves: damned." Alcino knows he isn't talking to himself in the slow late afternoon hours, the time for saying Hail-Marys.

"Amen," agree the exalted hearts.

Amen, Amen, the son-of-a-bitch.

In the general store we all cross ourselves as though we were inside a sacred convent, a room containing the holy images from all the funerals that ever were. And God save us from the words. Each sigh is full of sweet opportunity to be seized and cherished, redolent of palm oil, chewing tobacco, creosote and rum.

"Alcino, sing the song about White-Socks," the cry crosses the wide square in a straight line. The man at the door looks back into the general store. Everyone is laughing, nobody thinks of the dead any more. Three cheers for the madman.

"White-Socks is like the moon, /Half-a-house is

half-a-tune,/ the empty tunes my heart has known..." Pedro Infante, the store-keeper, sings jovially. He has managed to bring in the verses Alcino made up on the day the mare White-Socks died.

Another customer unloads his burden and relaxes. "Pour me a drink, Pedro. Put it on my bill."

The general store lights up: Nobody is dead now.

"Where're the women, Pedro? How is it women never come in this joint?"

"This is a serious place of business."

Buttocks swaying as he goes after the glass. The torso insinuating a bump-and-grind movement. Before taking a long swallow of rum, the man sings:

"A land of decent women and hard-working me-en..."

The others can't understand so much merriment. But they are already involved, like it or not.

"How do you suppose the fool gets along, now that the mare's dead?" says the rum-drinker, covering the rim of his glass with his open hand. Now it's he who sings, "White-Socks is like the moon..."

"He goes after the jenny-asses, just like you," says a man who gets up and asks for two fingers' worth of rum in a glass. "Just two fingers' worth."

"Watch it there, I'm a married man."

"Married to who? Violet the she-ass?" The dog-pack snarls, waiting to chew on the bone.

"Married, yeah, but only because you were shotgunned. Every man has the whore he deserves."

"Throw the first stone. Throw it." The accused looks at the bottom of his glass. He is going to order another drink. "What I really want to know is how Alcino manages nowadays. The mare died, didn't she?"

16

"Yeah. Wasn't it about then he started preaching sermons?"

"Well, it isn't my fault the mare died."

"Nobody's saying it's your fault."

"But I have to listen to his sermons. It's enough to try a man's patience."

"The worst thing was a woman who agreed to marry him."

"Good thing she changed her mind in time."

"White-Socks has changed her mind too, in the vultures' bellies."

"Don't you believe it! The mare died groaning with pleasure. If animals could talk, White-Socks would have said, before she closed her eyes forever, 'Alcino, I can die happy. Because I never knew another horse like you.' "

"And it's true, she didn't."

Figures sculpted in the hot air of the afternoon. Other people's business is like a cooling breeze. Today we lighten our spirits at the madman's expense. Tomorrow it will be someone else, but it matters little: we're still alive.

"One day I surprised Alcino on top of her," continues the man who was last to speak. "The mare was nibbling a branch and grinding her teeth with satisfaction."

At that time the crazy man wasn't crazy yet and when he saw me he said, "Look here, you shameless thug, I'm not doing what you think. If you keep on thinking what you're thinking, I'm going to smash your head with this stick."

The whole general store shakes. "Did you see what size the stick was?"

"Not me, I ran away."

Bottles dance on the shelves. Pedro Infante tries to

control them. One good laugh is enough to make the whole place fall apart.

"You must look a lot like the woman who married him."

They all remembered, didn't they?

A woman fleeing faster than a streak of lightning through a manioc patch. Behind her, the fury of a naked man who stumbles and trips among the plants, victim of his own erect stalk. They look like two utter lunatics. The woman, the faster of the two, has the wilder appearance. She jumps the fence and escapes her pursuer, without looking back. "Wait, wait!" he cries. "Don't run away, calm down!" The street urchins shout, "Catch her, catch her!" They had been spying on the two from the beginning, eyes squinting through cracks and ears glued to the walls. They wondered what the outcome of it all would be. They didn't have to wait long.

Alcino's marriage didn't last beyond the first night. It ended at the exact moment he took off his clothes and stretched out belly-up on the bed. In his urgency, he had forgotten to put out the lantern, or perhaps that wasn't the reason he had left it on. Maybe he wanted to see close up what a woman's body looked like. And that lantern was his ruin. The woman didn't even get undressed. Seeing what was in store for her, she ran for dear life. They say he started to go crazy from that night on.

Everybody knew Alcino had enormous parts. He never wore underwear. Moreover, he always wore trousers made of very thin cloth, tied at the waist with a string as if they were pyjamas. And as if that weren't enough, the trousers were very tight and never reached more than halfway down his shins. Women would never look at him below the waist.

The men, less discreet, spread the rumor that he was the son of a donkey.

On nights when his attacks of lunacy come, he invents difficult words that nobody understands. Nobody knows where Alcino learned so many long words. But we don't pay much attention to him now.

"He's like that because he should have been a priest but no one put him in the seminary," say the pious ladies of the church.

"He's like that because he jacks off so much," say the men in the general store.

"Pedro, lend me your mare. I'm needing it bad today."

"How much you give me for her?"

"Whatever you say."

"So let's see your money."

"Put it on the bill."

It almost seemed as if nothing had happened, that that was how life was: Mass once in a while, market day every week, a holy pilgrimage once a year, harvest according to the winter rains and so it goes, pour me another one, until a man came in. A prudent man of few words, or at least the kind of words that were circulating among the drinkers. We stopped laughing, maybe because he was old, a very old, old man. He said,

"It's hard to believe. It's one of those things you see, you know it's true and that it really happened, but you don't want to believe it. Why, only yesterday I was here, under this very roof, this very light above my head, and I heard music coming from up yonder in the direction of the church. I went and looked out of the door, and saw it was Nelo coming. He had his radio on, tuned in to the Sociedade station in Salvador. He was walking slowly and I thought: a capitalist, a man from the capital cities, never in a hurry. I went out to meet him, to see if what my eyes perceived was real or if it was just an illusion. I walked with my head down, because Nelo's silver hair blinded the eyes more than the sun shining in a mirror. We met right there in the middle of the square. Now let me tell you: the thing I most appreciate in a person is when that person knows how to use his words. I put my hand on Nelo's shoulder, but not making a nuisance of myself, and said, 'Come to look over the old place, eh?' I don't think Nelo heard that bit, but when he turned the radio down, I said, 'Everything in tune, is it?' I was very proud of the way he answered, and I swear by this light that shines on me, there isn't a man here who could talk the way he did. Nelo said to me: 'Friend, nowadays it's not like it was in the old times. Things have changed one by one, because I've been impetuous. Now...now I am a citizen of the developed world.' Before he even finished speaking I was already saying, 'Thank you, Nelo. Thank you very much.' I think he was proud of me too, or he wouldn't have said, 'You can always count on me.' It's hard to believe that a man like that could...I don't even like to think about it.''

What's the matter with these old geezers? All they can do is preach sermons—thinks the rum-drinker, the most daring of the men. If he had said it out loud, the others would have had a good laugh. He kept quiet. The store was not the same.

But the afternoon remained exactly the same, as blue as ever. Soon the sky would be streaked, beginning to turn the red that has to come before nightfall, and the fear it brings. The men's hearts were heavier than the tolling of the great church bell.

Chorus: "Nelo was a man of no faith."

His defender (the old man) wasn't going to carry that insult home. He said: "Only God knows what goes on in a person's mind."

The others said nothing.


# V


Nelo and I were walking along in the direction of the farm, hanging on to each other. We were going to the house where we were born—but which hadn't belonged to the family for years. Nelo was dripping with sweat, but I couldn't take his arm off my shoulder: he was so drunk that he kept stumbling. We would take a step or two and then stop. To talk.

"Totonhim...you are Totonhim, aren't you?"

He drew out the name with a São Paulo accent. I felt like telling him that folks here don't trust people who talk that way. To his face, they'd admire his new accent, but behind his back...

"Yes, I'm Totonhim."

"So that means you're my brother."

"Of course we're brothers."

"If you're my brother, then you're my friend, right?"

"Right."

"So about-face. Take me to my wife's house."

"But I don't know where your wife's house is."

"It must be in Itaquera. Or in Itaim."

"Where the devil's that?"

"Near São Miguel Paulista."

The girl at the post office is always saying, "Junco. Capital: São Miguel Paulista." The reference couldn't have been more timely.

"I didn't know you were married."

"S-h-h-h" he put a finger to his mouth. "I'm going to tell you a secret, Totonhim. Swear you won't tell anybody?"

"I swear."

"You have a niece and a nephew."

His two kids, plus six others, plus four others, plus two others, how many nieces and nephews do I have altogether? I've lost track.

"What are their names?"

"Robertinho and Eliane. The boy is eight and the girl, seven. How I miss them! It's been more than a year since I saw them."

"But you've only been here three weeks."

"Never mind that. Help me."

"We're in Junco, man. How many times in your life have you walked down this road? Do you remember?"

"With a milk can on my head and my shoes strung around my neck. That was our life: deliver the milk, then look for a house where we could wash our feet. You used to do that too, didn't you?"

"Not so much. There was a big gap between us. So many kids... It was hard on you being the oldest, wasn't it?"

"Call a taxi, man. I'll pay, I don't care what it costs."

"The only taxi you'll find here is a donkey's back."

"I don't think you're Totonhim."

"I'm Totonhim."

"Then help me. I need to find my wife and kids. I'll

kill her and you can help me bring the kids back. If I catch that son-of-a-bitch, that Baiano—"

"We're all Baianos, this is the state of Bahia."

"But he's a mean half-breed. He robbed me of everything I had. What's worse, he's my cousin."

"Who are you talking about?"

"Oh, no. Totonhim, I won't tell you that. Let's run underneath the trees."

"Why?"

"Because of the rain."

"What rain?"

"I can tell you're not Totonhim."

"Yes, I am Totonhim."

"It's raining, Totonhim."

"The sun's shining hot enough to fry an egg."

"Then it's raining and sunshining at the same time."

"I don't see any rain."

"I see green rain in front of my eyes, Totonhim. I see it, and if I see it, I'm not making it up."

So I looked through the open space between his eye and the green lens of his glasses. I said:

"You're right. But it's only a sprinkle. Let's just keep walking anyway."

"Oh, no. No, we don't. I don't want to get wet, because my suit will fade. This is the only one I brought. But I brought a lot shirts, didn't I?"

"I didn't look in your suitcase." I really wanted to change the subject, so he'd stop talking about the rain.

"When we get back I'll show you. That is, if you're really Totonhim."

"I am Totonhim."

"Then take me to my wife's house."

"She's in São Paulo, Nelo. And São Paulo is a hell of a long way from here."

"She's in Itaquera or Itaim, I told you. The other side of São Miguel Paulista."

"Right."

"Dammit, call a taxi."

"We're almost there. Look, there's the house, it's still there."

Nelo took his arm from my shoulder and walked forward a few steps, so I wouldn't see him cleaning his glasses. We were at the top of the hill on the road that runs down between two sections of *macambira*-wood fence, one of which he had helped put up, digging the postholes along with the hired hands. Papa was always telling about this, saying how Nelo was the best of all his children. "He was the only one who took after me," he would lament, in the face of our unwillingness to work with a hoe. Even so, we were all to spend the rest of our lives referring to that house as ours, especially Papa who, having left it once and for all, never had the courage to look back.

"You were right, Totonhim. It wasn't raining at all."

Now he was gazing at the house and fields as if he were visiting the grave of someone he had loved very much—and the effect of what he saw must have been strong, for he already seemed less drunk than before.

"Shall we go back?"

"Don't you want to go the rest of the way? The gate is just down there."

"I know. But let's leave it for another day."

"But since we've come this far—"

"Not today," he said and started walking on ahead of me, back toward town.

Silent and closed: locked.

# VI

"It was an evil spell," said Mama.

# VII

They arrived while the street lights were still on, which meant that it wasn't yet ten o'clock. It meant that the jeep from the Mayor's office must have gone and come back in a hurry. And from here to Feira de Santana is a long ride, over unpaved roads. Undoubtedly, the driver knew the best short-cuts to take. Like it or not, knowing a mayor can be useful.

He's their son. Let them get here and make their own arrangements for the funeral, I thought as I waited. What a wait. If the world kept moving with the slowness of that afternoon, it would never end. I made plans, rehearsed words. The orange-leaf tea that Zé the druggist kept giving me, one cup after another to keep me calm, was too sweet; but I was going to need to be very calm indeed when Papa and Mama arrived. I would have to explain everything to them from the very beginning. I was going to have to be one of the pallbearers. But I wouldn't be able to tell them why Nelo hadn't been to visit them in Feira de Santana, since the bus from São Paulo stops there first.

Far worse, however, was the sergeant and his unanswered questions. He wanted the impossible: for me to tell him why my brother had done what he did. At least

Zé the druggist, our doctor on this and all occasions, was there with me. If it hadn't been for him, the police sergeant would have bothered me even more than he did, although his stupid interrogation didn't have the slightest importance in the face of what was really upsetting me. At that exact moment I was asking myself if Papa would make the coffin. And it wasn't an irrelevant question.

The last coffin he had made was for another man who hanged himself, a relative of ours whom we found swinging from the branch of a *barauna* tree on our very own land. To this day it takes courage to pass under that tree after sunset. I remember it perfectly: Papa cut the rope and held the body in his arms, the way he used to carry one of us to bed after we had already fallen asleep. He laid the dead man carefully on the ground and asked us to bring him some boards and his tools. He also asked for a bottle of rum. He washed his hands in rum, took a swig out of the bottle, and set to work. When he got home he said, "At least the vultures won't eat the poor devil."

"He won't be eaten by vultures," I say, my thoughts already on something else: what if Papa takes a long time to get here and Nelo starts to stink? I can't let Nelo stink.

"The boy's nervous, Sergeant," explains Zé the druggist. "Don't you think it would be better to cut down the body? In cases like this there's never much of an explanation."

It was a relief to hear that. Zé might have added, Look, Sergeant, sir, you've only been the police officer here a short time. You come from Salvador, from the state capital, and you don't know the many mysteries of this place. Let me tell you: ever since I moved here to start my little pharmacy and married a Cruz girl and had a string of kids,

26

I've seen labor pains close up, and almost every time I got there too late, only to hear a baby crying over a dead mother's body. Let's change the subject, sir. We've talked enough.

Motionless in the dusty old armchair left over from a past unknown to him, the sergeant seemed to converse with the oval photograph, also dusty, of my grandfather. Nelo, the rope still around his neck, receives the patriarch's silent gaze. Mama used to say it was Nelo who tied Grandfather's tie for him the day Papa took that picture. "He gave my little Nelo a penny, patted him on the head and said, 'A damned smart little fellow. You're going to be somebody one day, son.' " That was what the old lady used to tell us all the time, her mouth full of pride and chewing tobacco.

I know now that a man can go crazy and then return to normal. Here they say it's the Devil who enters his body. I can't say how long the Devil stayed in my body because at that time I didn't have a watch. And if I did, I wouldn't have had the patience to measure the time that madness lasted. Yes, it was madness.

Because the memory of those things—the knot in the necktie, the penny given as a reward, Mama, everything—made me get up and stand in front of my dead brother, challenging him to fight.

"Did you come back here just to do this to me? You had all of Brazil to do it in, but you came here and chose this room! Wake up, you son-of-a-bitch!"

I went up to Nelo, ready to hit him. But Zé the druggist pinned back my arms, telling me to calm down. That was when he called the sergeant aside into another room for a private conversation. I sat down again, without the nerve to look at the other two men. I covered my face with my hands, like an old lady who hides herself beneath a black veil upon entering church. It was a mixture of regret, shame and despair. I began to cry.

When the two men came back into the room, one of them asked me for the medical prescription that Nelo always carried in his pocket. I answered that I didn't even know of a medical prescription he carried around in his pocket. "But I know," said the druggist.

It was true. The prescription was in his wallet, an old empty wallet. I mean there was no money in it. It was stuffed with documents, lottery-ticket stubs, a letter, and an old snapshot of two smiling children. I recognized Mama's old pothook handwriting on the letter, even before looking at the return address. On the back of the snapshot was written "Papa, never forget us. Robertinho and Eliane." The handwriting was an adult's, small and rounded, the letters leaning backward. A woman's handwriting.

And that was all except for the clothes on his back. As if he had been thinking of going out, as if the idea of dying hadn't been premeditated. Who will want to inherit the clothes? There will be no lack of candidates for the transistor radio, the watch and the glasses. I'll keep the glasses myself. A fine memento.

"This medicine is for the nerves," I heard Zé the druggist say, pointing to a greasy word among other words equally illegible to a layman's eyes.

"I know, I know," said the sergeant, considering the case closed. "I know, I know."

He left and we stayed there: myself, the druggist, the dead man and my grandfather's picture. I thought of a

pretty rhyme the sergeant could have delivered, had he had
better manners or been capable of a lighthearted farewell:

*Good-bye.*

*Untie the rope.*

*Go to hell without a hope.*

The prescription was a secret, and Zé had promised
himself that he wouldn't tell anyone about it, not even his
own wife, a Cruz girl, that is to say, our cousin.

We can't always keep our promises, he would say now.
Besides, who's going to pay the bill?

"I had to send away to Alagoinhas for the medicine,
with money out of my own pocket. When I delivered your
brother's order he said, 'Zé, can I buy this on credit?
Thanks, friend. Open an account for me. We'll settle up
later.' "

"Well, then he's the one to settle up with."

"Where? In hell? Don't fool around with me."

We had the body in our arms, laying it on the cool
tiles of the floor. Nelo's eyes were wide open. He was staring at the ceiling without blinking. We covered up his body
from head to toe with a sheet.

"Wait for Judgement Day, Zé. Isn't that when we're
all going to settle our accounts?"

"Man, I'm no millionaire. You know that."

He was no longer the mild, well-mannered man he
had been before, that is, the man who had come here on
donkeyback from Irara, an infinitely more civilized place.
Besides his supply of drugs, he had brought in his sad-
dlebags a large stock of words we didn't know, until we
realized that they were words we did know, only correctly
pronounced. That was enough, in the beginning, for us
to consider him stuck-up.

"Talk to Papa about it, Zé," I say, already preparing to leave.

"I guess that's all I can do. You don't have any money either, right?"

Zé had a good heart. Nobody left his pharmacy without the medicine they needed, whether they had money to pay for it or not. We discovered our mistake: he wasn't stuck-up. In time, however, we had cause to doubt his competence. To expect someone to be saved through his ministrations was just as improbable as predicting whether the next winter would be a good or a bad one. His defense: they only come to me when they're already past help.

In addition to the blind belief that all sickness could be cured with medicines—instead of herbal teas and prayers—what seemed to keep him going was his faith in being able to extend credit to everyone, because people wouldn't fail to pay if their health was involved, although they might fail in other things. Nelo probably didn't even suspect all this when he went into the drugstore and explained his problem.

"Zé, I'm going to need your help. I want a few little things."

The druggist, standing behind the counter, consulted the list of people who ought to contribute to the founding of a new secondary school and was happy to see that one name was still missing.

"High school? Are you kidding? What's all this, Zé?"

"It's progress. Whatever you want to give will be fine," said Zé. "It's for the common good. Your brother is going to be one of the teachers, didn't he tell you?"

"Take this for now. Later I'll give more."

"Every bit helps," said Zé, who still didn't know the

truth: that was the last money he had, all that was left of his imagined fortune.

Then he showed Zé the prescription and placed his order. And in the same way that the blood and feces samples taken for examination had stripped him naked in his own eyes some time ago, his body was now utterly exposed to the druggist's knowledge: the medicines were for syphilis and intestinal worms. He needed some tranquilizers, too, because he was very nervous these days—the same nervousness that had once made him tear out a sink from the wall and smash it to pieces, like a clay pot. The other item he ordered was the secret that Zé the druggist, a reliable man and, in fact, his cousin, would keep for the rest of his life.

"Zé..." I was locking the door of the house after us. "I'll pay the bill. Wait till the end of the month. As soon as I get my salary from the Mayor's office, I'll pay you."

"All right," said the druggist. "I won't say anything to your father."

I went down to the general store.

There, they were asking what had happened the night Nelo chased after the queer.


# VIII

It was like this.

They made a deal. They would beat up the punk who, besides being queer, had been hanging around one of Pedro Infante's sisters. So Pedro had the idea. Nelo's part would be to lure him out onto the sidewalk in front of the church after everyone was in bed.

"It's no worse than doing it with a donkey," said Pedro, who had been born and raised in the town, and therefore was smarter than Nelo, a boy from the farm.

"What if Mama finds out?"

"Stop being a pain in the ass. Nobody's going to tell her." Pedro shuffled the bills stolen from the drawer of the general store, which back then belonged to his father.

So they had it all set up. The two of them were already undressed when the others arrived. The queer, stark naked and carrying his clothes, tried to run away. They ran after him and caught him. Pedro Infante put out one of the boy's eyes with his belt buckle. The next day he stole some more money, gave it to the boy and told him to get lost. He disappeared, nobody knew where. But when Pedro's father noticed the money was missing, Pedro put all the blame on Nelo. Papa paid for the losses to clear the family name.

Nelo got two thrashings: one from Papa, one from Mama.

And he stopped speaking to Pedro Infante.

# IX

The news spread like wildfire—Junco tongues have no restraint whatsoever—the owner of the general store was drunk. It was the second important news item of the day. Never in his life had he touched a single drop. The Devil gloats over one more condemned sinner.

Pedro Infante knew now: dirty deals are not undone with time, because God, the Father of forgetfulness, doesn't let sin go unpunished. Pedro actually believed the opposite when he learned that Nelo was back, but it was a vain belief, and now Pedro was going to drink until he dropped. He needed to wash away the old spot, but it wasn't forgiveness he could see in the bottom of his glass, nor simply a tot of vermouth mixed with rotgut rum. He saw drops of blood, the stains of his damnation. So Pedro didn't appreciate the sergeant's coming in and asking, "Is this where they're holding the wake?"

Here he is again: a man who could be just like everyone else were it not for the authority conferred on him by that gun. There are those who suspect that the sergeant doesn't even take off his pistol to go to sleep. But they don't voice their suspicions.

"The strength that poor devil must have had."

Words of compassion? Yes, yes, brothers. Men aren't always so bad, even the sergeant, who is an atheist.

Better not trust him—the doubt is stamped on the weathered face of the old farmer, the one who finds it hard to believe. One can read on his forehead: I don't like this officer. I never saw him at Mass.

"There's one thing I don't understand. Why is it so many people hang themselves around here?"

"Pardon me, but you'd better ask God, don't ask me," the old man informs him.

Pedro Infante crosses himself, thinking: Why have you done this to me, you bastard?

Just then a glass slips out of his hand, rolls onto the floor but doesn't break. A bad sign. Pedro bends over warily and picks it up. Night is falling, and it's at night that the dead come back. Pedro hits the counter three times with his fist. He has nothing to say. Nor does he know what to do.

"You seeing ghosts, man?" the sergeant laughs, the

33

only one there still able to do so.

"Let the demons come—all of 'em," Pedro feigns toughness, getting himself a new glass. "My body is proof against them."

But this time, the owner of the general store doesn't smile to show off the gold teeth that distinguish him from other members of the human race.

It was Dr. Walter Robatto, Jr., who put all that gold in his mouth. The famous dental surgeon of J.J. Seabra Square, Alagoinhas, Bahia. Walter with a *w*, Robatto with two *t*'s. "A man with a name like that is born distinguished," Pedro came back saying, through his millionaire smile. "Now a vulgar name like Cruz holds no future for anyone. It's downright defeating to be born with a name that's only fit for the torment of Our Lord. I'm going to change my name."

And he did. He became Pedro Batista Lopes instead of Pedro Batista da Cruz. Infante was a nickname.

"How did that story go about the queer?" The atmosphere thickens. There's a time for jokes, the old man must be thinking, with all the older men. The owner of the general store agrees:

"What story is that, Sergeant?"

"Don't pretend you've forgotten, man. You can't have lost your memory from one day to the next. We even had a good laugh over it."

"For the love of God, Sergeant. Today's not the day to dig up such things."

"Where's your balls, Pedro? Only fit to hold up your dick when you pee?"

"Will you just shut up, dammit."

The rum was boiling behind Pedro Infante's fair skin.

34

He was a man with many odd habits. He never went out in the sun without covering the backs of his hands with his shirt-cuffs and turning up his collar to protect his neck. He took no chances whatsoever: at any hour of the day one might meet him with his umbrella open so as not to get burned even if he was only walking from the store to his house. We would see him like that on horseback, too, going toward his father's farmlands, which he inherited when old Jeremiah passed on, leaving him a store full of stock that was already paid for, since old Jeremiah wasn't a man to buy things on credit. Nobody here had better luck than Pedro Infante. Even when the subject of women became an obsession, his horse still turned up at the right address after traveling leagues and leagues through remote country. A view of fertile fields from the veranda. Good-looking girls eyeing the road, who knew very well how to count their own head of cattle. The horseman Pedro Infante, questing through valleys and underbrush, was to return with his beloved on the saddle behind him. He would later give her five children, proving to the world that pale skin has nothing to do with masculinity. The girl was very pretty, and her father was another who didn't buy on credit.

And perhaps it was the memory of times in which men were worth something because they had cattle and gave their word, that made the old weather-worn farmer raise his voice, putting an end to the discussion between Pedro Infante and the sergeant.

"My friends," the old man stood up—hat in hand, because a respectable man doesn't go inside a church or speak to another man with a hat on his head—"I want to say to you all that for me, today is as sad as Good Friday. Our kinsman, our fellow citizen, and the son of a family that deserves our deepest respect, has finally given in to the temptations of the Devil. Friends, today is no day for misunderstandings. It would be better if we all prayed for the soul of that poor creature. That's all I ask. Leave off fooling and joking. We all have to acknowledge God.''

The old man sat down again on his stool and peace reigned in the store once more. He turned to me:

"What time does your father get here?''

I told him I didn't know, but that he was sure to be on his way already, and my answer at least served to block out a comment of the sergeant's. He was leaning against the wall opposite us, and was only a short distance away. "You're a funny crowd,'' was what he said, but I couldn't understand what he meant by it.

Losing interest in the living and the dead, the sergeant settled his back against the counter, crossed his legs and stared out at the empty square, as if he were wanting to discover some secret beneath its hard-packed dirt, behind the houses, beyond the Cruzeiro das Montes and the Big Hill, the same hill over which the road led away from the fields to São Paulo. From that hill he had first set eyes on Junco six months ago. We knew nothing at all about him, except that he didn't say much, but had the right to use force stamped on his short-sleeved khaki shirt. He'd arrived with his wife and children in the jeep of the old National Union of Democrats, which now had a new name, to wash the dirty political linen with his own hands. The defeated Social Democratic Party hacks handed over the job to him, tucked their tails between their legs and went off to plant beans. But the new police sergeant wasn't about to be branded a nobody. His opening performance took place on a market day, when the streets of the town were full.

The sergeant caught some petty thief, the kind that steals candy from newspaper stands, hoisted him up onto a large empty barrel and opened the jailhouse door and windows wide so everyone could appreciate his professional skills. The message was clear; and, his warning given, a new era was to begin in a town that had always been the same day after day. People now piled together at the sergeant's window to watch the eight o'clock evening soap opera on television. A television!—only a man from the capital could have brought us such a marvel. Dances on Saturday nights, not the customary country dances, but Robert Carlos on the battery-operated record player. We forgot the horse races over the dirt roads, our old Sunday afternoon entertainment: now we had the Married Men's soccer team playing against the Single Men's, on the field that the sergeant himself had prepared with hoe and scythe. We even made plans for matching the Junco Municipal Team against those from Inhambupe, Irara, and Serrinha. Even the Alagoinhas Athletic team was mentioned, and the most daring spoke of drafting an invitation to the Bahia Sport Club team of Salvador—the sergeant would, of course, add the finishing touches.

All this excitement had shaken us from the monotony of our lives; we even began to talk of looking for a progressive candidate for the next election. And this was the Junco that Nelo found after his twenty years' absence. Yet his arrival brought a subtle slowdown in the progress we had seen—for, with no apparent reason, the sergeant began to wilt, to grow apathetic. People wondered: was there an unconfessable disease, an evil spell? They even blamed the envy of the old Social Democratic Party, now also under another name, for holding Junco back from achieving true development.

"Well, Sergeant? Will we be having the cowboys' festival or not?"

"Sure we are."

"But when?"

"One of these days."

"Don't forget you promised."

The shadow of the church is touching the shadow of the houses in the middle of the square. Soon it will be dark. What if Papa doesn't get here? I look at the sergeant. He continues to scrutinize the ground of the square. Just staring down, with no word or expression.

I know he wanted to kill my brother, I know it. Ever since the day his wife asked who was the man sitting on the sidewalk outside the church. She said he was handsome. And then—but don't think about it any more, Sergeant. All you lost was the chance to kill a man, a man who was dead already, as it turned out.


# X


They grabbed me by the ears and neck and hit my head against the curbstone. I screamed. I hoped my scream would fill the deserted street, climb the walls of the buildings, enter the apartments, wake up men, women and children, split open the heavy black clouds of the city of São Paulo and disturb the sleep of God: "Help! They're killing me!"

A light came on after my third scream and a man appeared at a window above. He stood there watching. They kept on smashing my head against the curb. The light pierced my eyes, hard and penetrating, like the pain. Was it a spotlight, a torch, or a star? Just at that moment Papa's hand appeared, offering me a hat. "Cover your head, then it won't hurt so much." I tried to stretch out my arm, but just as I was about to take the hat in my hand, they hit me again.

"You told on me, Totonhim. Now look what happened. You shitty stoolpidgeon!"

They laughed.

I felt a cold barrel tickling my earlobe.

"Shall I finish him off?"

"Wait a minute."

"What'll we do with him afterwards?"

"Throw his carcass in the Tietê River."

Papa disappeared under the water. The hat floated along on the current. Between the peaceful banks, dark, stinking water. Tietanic water.

Cold winds, strong men: from the North and the South.

Hold your nose and good luck.

"I didn't do anything, I swear to God."

Pieces of my skull scattered over the sidewalk. They kept on hitting me.

"Hand over the money, you thief!"

"I'm not a thief. You can kill me, but I'm no thief."

"So show me your identity papers."

"I left them at home, I told you."

At first it was only a dream. I was running toward the bus terminal when they cried, "Stop, thief!" I didn't hear them. But even if I had, I would never have imagined they were yelling at me. I kept on running and again they cried, "Stop, thief!" I dodged cars, jostled into people, bumped against lampposts, still running. I couldn't let the bus leave Clovis Square without seeing if the woman and two children waiting in line were who I thought they were. "Stop, thief!"—this time it was very close and I thought, somebody must have robbed a shopkeeper; and this bus is stealing my wife and kids. I forced my legs to go faster, advancing a few yards, but it made no difference; the bus had left. I stopped running, my chest nearly bursting, a huge pain in my heart. They grabbed me.

"Come back, come back!" I struggle, kick, plead. "I'm getting myself straightened out, I'm earning money again, I'm doing business, I buy clothes here and sell them in the north of Paraná—" I stumble among the suitcases, a barricade of suitcases. "Last week I earned a lot of money in Londrina. I stopped drinking. Now I'm working hard, come back!"—a kick in the belly, a gasping shudder. "Come back, I'll be a different man, I'll be another Nelo, forgive me, come back!" A hard shove. They're going through my pockets, where's the gun? "I can't stand it any more, I want to see my kids, I want to wake up every morning and see my kids—" rough hands search me, slap me in the dizzying headlights. People crowd around; a thief's been caught, everyone wants to see what's going on. "Come back, come back, for the love of God!"

I begin to cry.

"Confess—you were going to kidnap the children."

"Confess—you were going to kill your wife."

Well, hello, Zé the trumpet player, what an honor. To what do I owe this pleasant surprise? It was him, the Baiano. I'd helped him get the first job he ever had. He was a bus conductor on the Penha-São Miguel Paulista line. After that he joined the police. After that he took my wife and two kids. "Where's the revolver you bought to kill me with?" Zé frisks me, pats my cheek, then slaps me hard. By some miracle, I manage to knee him in the belly. Then they grab me by the ears and the neck and pound my head against the sidewalk.

"Confess—you're a thief."

"Confess—you're a bum."

I say No, no, no.

A wide avenue running along the banks of the Tietê River. Dark, deep waters. Tietanic waters. At the bottom, the city of São Paulo.

They kept on hitting me and it was very late and there was nobody left in the street and the man who had turned on the light and come to the window did nothing but watch, and I screamed: "It's a lie! It's all a lie!"

"Confess, cuckold."

Papa appeared again—just his hand, now without the hat. Papa's hand came flying towards me and I thought: he's going to strangle me. I closed my eyes.

No, no, no, no.

In the distance sirens whine: here comes the Rescue Squad. Their sound grows closer and closer—they've come to help me. But the ambulances go by without stopping. One of the policemen has ordered them to go on.

"Confess, cuckold."

They're playing a Bolero; I'm dancing. At the front of the stage is Zé the trumpet player, skinny and writhing, his coat open and his shirt soaked with sweat. A Saturday night dance in Itaquera. People circulate on the dance floor. The room revolves. My head spins. "Are you from around here?" she whispers, soft and luminous, like the music. "No, I live in São Miguel Paulista." Wait, be quiet. Rings of white clouds; I step on the clouds, I step on her foot. Embarrassment: "Excuse me." No, no, it didn't matter, it was her fault, it had been a long time since she had danced. Same with me. Oh, not at all, you dance beautifully. This time my legs refuse to hold me up, I'm lost. "That guy can really play," she says. "He's my cousin," I reply. Zé the bus conductor played the trumpet on Saturdays at the dances round about. Then he joined the police and forgot about the trumpet. At intermission time he came to our table, the girl was already with me at the table and I said, May I have the pleasure of introducing you to the greatest musician in Junco and she laughed and asked where the devil is that, you mean you're Baianos, you don't look like Baianos, you don't have yellow faces and spots and your hair is nice and straight. My head spins, the world spins, I embrace her, the smell of a woman, her woman's body, I hold her close forever, forever.

They're pissing on my face, and I'm swimming in the stream near our house, the waters of that stream flow into the Inhambupe River, which flows into the Tietê. I hold onto a *mulungu* trunk so as not to drown, kicking my legs slowly in the water, unhurried, unafraid of drowning. The trunk slips out of my grasp and I sink to the bottom; the mud sucks at my face. I fight my way up to the surface. I'm drowning: "Help me!"

"Confess, cuckold."

A pair of horns grows on my forehead and turns into a huge flowering branch. Beautiful red flowers, radiant in the morning sunlight. Now the branch becomes heavy, I can't bear to stand up. I fall. "Chop the goddamn thing off."

"We're in no hurry," they say.

The piss runs hot and stinking down my face, it's the rain God sent at the right time—you see, we were right to plant on St. Joseph's Day. I helped Papa plant the beans and corn; me, Mama, the girls and the hired men, and every day I would get up a little earlier, to see if the seeds had sprouted. It was pretty to see the seeds come up, and even better to see the plants grow, the leaves open, dewy in the early morning.

"Where did you hide the money, thief?"

No, no, no, no.

I piss: beer. I dream: relief.

They relieve themselves on me, and it refreshes me. They can't piss and beat me at the same time.

Papa, I hope things get better. I think about that all the time. I hope things get better. Our fields were green once, I know. Now we have no fields left. I need to send money for you to buy back the house and the farm you sold. I hope things get better.

I play the lottery every week. I bet, I lose, I bet, I lose. I never win. I work hard, I try to reform myself, I even stopped stealing—I mean, I stopped drinking.

I piss: water. I dream: calm.

How many of them are there? I don't know. I can't see them. Maybe a dozen. The worst one of all is that Zé who used to be Zé the trumpet player. Now they're pissing two by two. In my face. Even my cousin, the Baiano.

I planted the fig tree beside the door, it must be a big tree by now. I planted five cashew nuts in the manioc patch; five cashew trees came up. One day I'll send money for you to buy back our farm, Papa. If I had more money, I could make more. I want to, believe me, I want to.

I piss: medicine. Mainly for cows.

I can't open my eyes, but I feel I'm still alive.

"Get up, cuckold."

When she told her parents she was going to marry me, Mama, they were disgusted.

Baianos are niggers.

Baianos are poor.

Baianos are queers.

Baianos leave their wives and children and go back to Bahia.

But we were married anyway, and we had two kids. (Some day I'll send you a picture of your grandchildren.) Then she ran away with Zé the trumpet player and took my kids with her.

Zé is killing me. They're killing me. There must be a dozen men, armed and in uniform. Here, in the middle of the street. In the greatest of capital cities.

Money, money, money.

Grow up fast, little boy, so you can go to São Paulo.

Here I've lived a little and died a little every day. In the middle of the smoke, in the middle of the money. I don't know whether to stay or go. I don't know if I'm in São Paulo or Junco.

"Up, cuckold."

They order me to get up and do a square-dance like we used to do in the country. I can't, I'm falling down, I can't. They start hitting me again.

The man at the window has gone. He turned off the light and disappeared, back to bed.

São Paulo is a deserted city. A desert.

Another blow and I forget everything.

# XI

Papa takes off his hat, crosses himself and uncovers the dead man's head.

"What's done is done."

Then he asks me where the boards and tools are. He starts making the coffin.

# PART TWO

# The Land Casts Me Out

THE OLD MAN let the gate bang shut without looking back.

But he couldn't avoid the sound of its closing, the final impact. It sent a tremble through him that made his legs buckle, as though refusing to go. He thought: Women are lucky, they know how to cry.

Three fields, a house, a patch of manioc, a plow, an oxcart, horses, cattle and a dog. A wife, twelve children. The sound of the gate closing was a farewell to all that. He had been a man; now he wasn't anything. He had nothing left.

"Women are a curse. All they think about is the world's vanities. Their only use is to sin and ruin men."

His legs didn't want to go, but he had to. He had to get into the village and hitch a truck ride to Feira de Santana, this time for good.

"And it's all her fault," he kept thinking. "Because of her crazy ideas about living in a city and sending the kids to school. As if schoolwork can fill your belly."

If he looked back, he would see the great tree at the door, shading the porch—the tree that he, his wife and his oldest son had planted.

The son had gone off against his wishes, and never come back. He was still a boy when he left. That foolish wife of his had been in favor of it. She nagged him about it day and night, bedevilling the people for miles around with her ideas, until they all made visits to give him advice, asking, asking, asking, to let the boy go. Eventually he realized he couldn't win; he would have to witness his own bad luck with arms crossed from then on. Now apparently the son was ashamed of him, because he didn't answer his letters, or rather, his messages that his wife scrawled in her letters, since he, the old man, barely knew how to sign his name on election day, which was nothing to be ashamed of: everyone here was like that. As long as you knew how to vote, you didn't have to learn anything else. His writing was of another type, and he took pride in doing it well: brown lines upon the plowed earth, the beautiful soft earth, generous throughout the whole year when God sent rain. The best pen in the world is the handle of a hoe.

No, he didn't want to go to Feira de Santana. His wife and the children who were left would have to get along on their own. A man who really is a man doesn't accept scraps. He would go to São Paulo or Paraná, good lands where he could certainly find a farm to take care of as if he owned it.

And that was exactly the message he sent his son, the message repeated so often, unanswered so many times. It was true that once, in a letter to his mother, Nelo had said, "Tell Papa that down here it's very hard for an older man. He won't get used to it. São Paulo isn't what you think up there. For the love of God, get that idea out of his head."

This answer was no good, and the old man thought he understood why his son never again touched on the matter, never bothered to answer other messages. "He doesn't want me there, now he's so refined. I'm a farmer and don't have his newfangled ways. That's it.''

He had woken at his usual time, long before sunrise.
But, unlike other days, he wasn't in a hurry to get out of
bed. He pushed the faded blanket to one side—a dirty rag
to be inherited by someone with a painstaking wife disposed
to wash and rub the blanket many times until all the dirt
was out, who afterwards wouldn't be ashamed to cover
herself with it. He would leave the bed and mattress too.
Lice and dreams. Pleasure and pain. The fleas would
transmit his blood to his nephews (he would give it to his
brother) but fleas don't talk. No one would know what it
had been like. Only he and God really knew, the same God
who had given him twelve children, right there on that very
mattress—boys and girls who came out of their mother's
womb into the waiting hands of the Negress Tindole,
drunken, excitable and miraculous black midwife whose
services were paid for with sacks of beans. Twelve navel
cords buried in the yard. Twelve times he set off a dozen
firecrackers, his happiness exploding in the air, announcing
renewal.

Quiet in the darkness, the old man doesn't listen to
the day dawning outside. He strains to hear the sounds of
life he has lived inside this house. He doesn't hear a thing.
He calls:

"Nelo, Noemia, Gesito, Tonho, Adelaide! Wake up,
children. Come and say prayers.''

His hand explores the space beside him, occupied in
times past by another body. There is nothing there except
a yellowed, foul-smelling blanket. Yet still he doesn't come
back to reality, doesn't wake from his dream.

*Kyrie, eleison,*
*Christe, eleison.*
*Kyrie, eleison.*

He stops. It would be a sacrilege to continue. The litany wasn't meant to be prayed by one person alone: there had to be the responses. One voice leading, the others joining in—at least two voices. The more voices, the greater the certainty of the prayer being heard in the ears of Our Lord. He calls again for the children. As useless as to continue praying. Annoyed, he raises his voice, the fatherly sternness of bygone days:

"What's happening in this house? Come on, wake up."

He gets up and walks through the empty bedrooms; there are no more beds, nothing. He goes into the kitchen and starts a fire. He starts to make some coffee, then rejects the idea and throws water on the kindling to put out the flames. Since he is leaving, what is the point of coffee, of a fire in the stove? He goes out onto the veranda. The first rays of dawn are showing, the color gold. He will carry these mornings forever, will take in his eyes and in his soul the dawning of these days. Each one is a promise of new life, leaving the old day behind. He walks down to the stream and takes off his clothes. The clean greenish water reflects his naked body, shaded by soft, fine grass, *angolinha* grass that grows beside rivers. He bends down and touches the surface to see if it's very cold, and with wet fingertips makes the sign of the cross. He always crosses himself before entering the water, an old custom. Fear of drowning, fear of snakes. His face grows larger now that he is bent over. "Today's Friday, two more days to go," he says, scratching his beard. He will not shave it until Sunday. His father had done the same and his grandfather before that. Shave once a week. It was no use his wife complaining with her newfangled notions: "Man, you're not out in the fields! Go and shave that face!"

A man of mixed blood, still strong in spite of his white hair—that is what he sees in the water. The reflected face is like a full moon. Though dark-skinned, he has the straight hair of the whites. One of his daughters ran off with a kinky-haired man, oh what a headstrong girl. God made white people for other white people, and blacks for blacks. Black and white together didn't set well. A good thing his grandchildren had straight hair. According to what he'd heard, they resembled their mother, not their father. He stepped on the river bottom, and mud bubbled up his leg to the surface. His daughter had only done that because she knew he was against it. Determined to have her way no matter what, she went off on the back of a Negro's saddle. That day the rooster crowed at the wrong hour. The world had been taken over by blind tomfoolery. It was no good setting the dogs on them. When they got to see her, she was already lost for good. She was soon pregnant. Nobody listens.... When ruin comes, it's too late for patching and fixing. He dives in. A *caboclo* of the North, his arms are the color of the earth. Under the water he remembers the day he taught his oldest son to swim. He took a *mulungu* trunk and said: "Hold on here with both hands. Now push. The *mulungu* will always float, it won't ever sink. Kick your feet. That's it." It was the first time he had ever undressed in front of his son. "You sure have a lot of hair," half-ashamed, the boy watched his father out of the corner of his eye. "When you grow up, you'll be the same." That night he heard his son say to the other children, "Papa has a big pecker, with hair all around. I saw it." His wife

53

complained: her husband had done wrong. "See there? You shouldn't have undressed in front of the boy." He apologized: he hadn't wanted to dirty his clothes in the mud of the stream. She gave the boy a thrashing and said he'd get another if he talked about such things again. She was a pitiless woman, who beat her children until their skin was raw. Sometimes they would argue about it. He didn't approve of cruelty in any form, and was proud to think of himself as a father who would die without ever having struck one of his children. It was enough to raise his voice. They would hang their heads, ashamed, repenting whatever wrongdoing they had committed. But where had this good upbringing got them? His children grew up and went off, clutching their mother's skirts, forgetting the marks her switch had left on them.

Now the old man swims calmly in a crawl. After his body grows accustomed to it, the cold water is pleasant. He doesn't need to go anywhere; he wants to spend the rest of his life in the water. He might have done exactly that if the dog hadn't suddenly appeared, come into the water, and swum just like a man from one bank of the river to the other. He was no longer alone. What would he do with that pest? A tree. That was it, he would leave the dog tied to a tree. His brother could come and untie him later on, but then that no-good was likely to let the poor creature pine away from hunger and thirst—his brother had no feelings for people, much less animals. No, that wouldn't work. This was the second dog he'd had. The first he had to kill as it had been bitten by a dog that was rabid. When they heard the shots, his children had cried; it was enough to tear your heart out. But he had to do it. The dog would have gone mad too, which would have been worse. Should he shoot this one? He no longer had the shotgun; he had sold it at the town market last Monday. He was going to move to a city, there wouldn't be any birds there. Good-bye, quails, good-bye, woodcock. He couldn't do it with a club, his arms would give out. There was a little *Tatu*-brand ant killer left in the storage room. That was the solution. He looks at the dog and thinks: "Everyone's day comes some time. This is yours." He senses the dog's restlessness; the animal seems to have read his mind. But maybe it is something else. When he gets out of the water, the dog is rolling calmly on the grass. Now it barks and investigates a thicket, starting to draw away from it, then going back. The old man decides to take a closer look: a startled *jaracuçu* snake is coiled ready to strike. He dives in again quickly, heading toward the opposite bank, the *Tatu* ant killer forgotten. The best thing would be to give the dog some food inside the manioc-press shed, leave the door pulled to but not shut, and sneak away until he got past the gate and onto the road to town. That was what he would do. Just that.

An old Backlander, he wasn't strong, nor was he weak. But he could fell a hardwood tree and transform it in a matter of hours into an axle that would last a lifetime. When an oxcart passed, singing its creaking song down the road, he knew that somewhere, someone was announcing his fame as a master carpenter.

Yes, he was strong.

He came from a long line of cowmen and wasn't afraid of bandits, just as João da Cruz, the first *vaqueiro*, hadn't been afraid of the jungle or the wildcats in the days before Junco came into existence. João da Cruz, father of the place. The man who was driven by the drought all the way from Simão Dias, in Sergipe. He came bringing his wife and tribe of children, all of them starving. And it was right here in Junco that he found some flour to eat, and shelter—a rest after traveling hundreds of leagues on foot. At that time there was nothing here but a ranch belonging to the Baron of Geremoabo, a fair-faced man from the capital. After João da Cruz had eaten his fill, he began killing wildcats, and would have killed the Baron too, except that he never showed his face again.

He was strong because he was a Cruz. But he couldn't look ahead of him. He would see his father-in-law's house, imposing and solitary. Worse, he would hear his father-in-law's voice: "While I'm alive, I won't sell one square inch of land." He kept his word.

"They're wretches. Fools."

The old man was thinking again about his wife.

"You lit a spark inside," she had said.

It was the discovery of a mystery and the end of a despair. On that night, many months after their marriage (he was twenty-two, she seventeen) he finally learned the secret of the union between a man and a woman, the reason behind the symbolic new clothes, the veil and the wreath of flowers—the veil he had torn and spotted with blood during the urgent, clumsy satisfying of his pent-up animal desire. It was the beginning of an understanding: something that he knew happened with animals and people, but he hadn't known what it was like for the simple reason that he had never experienced it. Now you are a man, he might have said to himself. And upon becoming a man, you fathered a man child, he might have added, if he had known what he would come to find out nine months later.

She seemed to know something he didn't, she seemed to have been born knowing, and this was another mystery he could not comprehend.

"Women are born whores. They have to be kept on a short rein." That day he discovered a new feeling, something akin to jealousy.

"The downfall of the world began when women shortened their sleeves and their skirts to show off their bodies. Sin is the devourer of the world"—that's what he is thinking now, going down the road slowly and remembering his many daughters, lost among the city streets and far from him. He can't look to one side or to the other.

On one side he would see the abandoned house that had been his parents', and would feel sorrow. They had died, and were resting in heaven, in purgatory or in hell.

On the other side, he risked coming face to face with his brother, who had inherited their father's lands and now owned the farm that had been his.

"The money you got was just enough that nobody could say you gave the land away," his wife told him. "Man, you're the biggest fool the world has ever seen."

It was on the day that he had come to Feira de Santana with the news: the men from the bank were squeezing him. They were going to take over everything. Given a choice between the bank and his brother, he preferred to sell the property to his brother. Thus he could pay off the debt to the bank and still have a little left over to open a small business in Feira de Santana.

"Just what do you expect to be able to do here with that piddling amount?" His wife was right, as he would discover later, but that was the wrong time to complain.

What was done was done. He would go back home only to sign the papers and turn over the farm. That day he drank only a cup of coffee; he couldn't eat anything. He went out alone, wandering about the streets of the city, which he still didn't know properly, with the excuse of looking for a job. Maybe here someone might have heard what a good carpenter he was: he would have to find his way. But everything was so different. He didn't know anyone, none of his *compadres* walked through these streets or lived in these houses. He gave up at once and went into the first bar, where he ordered rum and started to talk with the customers. No, none of them knew where a man might get a job as a carpenter. Everybody there worked as mechanics or gas pump attendants. He kept on drinking, without eating anything, without moving from the spot. That night when he got home his wife complained about the hour. He turned on her as if to finish her off; but a child pushed between them. He grabbed his father's arms with all his strength—more strength than he could have imagined in a boy, saying,

"So hit her, Papa—you're such a man..."

He lowered his eyes and let his arms go limp, without resisting. He didn't have the courage to say or do a thing, although he knew that with a shove he could knock the boy to the floor.

The bank business had been another rotten mess. It was true that shortly before he died his father-in-law, hearing his request to be a co-signer of the promissory notes, had warned him: "*Compadre*, banks are a trap. Banks enslave men, like gambling and drink. Think about it carefully, *compadre*. You're borrowing money at interest to hire hands. Suppose you don't have a good crop? They'll take everything away from you.''

He had expected his father-in-law to say that banks were no good. But he was a hard man who never did anything for his sons, let alone for a son-in-law.

His brother kept him stirred up, as though foreseeing everything that would happen; for a long time his brother had dreamed of buying that land. If only his wife hadn't lost her head over this business of moving to the city and his children had stayed at home, he wouldn't have needed hired men, he wouldn't have needed money from any bank at all.

''It's her fault,'' he thought again, remembering the first trip they had taken together to a big town.

They were going to make a pilgrimage to Our Lady of Candeias with the load of people who went every year, riding in the canvas-covered truck.

He would travel in the back, she in the cab.

He didn't like it.

He had heard many things about truck drivers—scandalous things, shameless things.

They always preferred the women to ride up in the cab, so they could have a little fun during the trip. Every time they changed gears, there was an opportunity to let a hand slip between a woman's legs. And then they would make their little jokes, start their little conversations.

They would tell dirty stories.

They would grab the women's hands.

They would do all sorts of things.

When they got back from the trip, that was all he could talk about for an entire month.

He wanted to know everything, he wanted to know

if she had worn her teeth out smiling at the driver.

The first time, she said the driver was nice.

The second time, she said the driver was very lively.

The third time, she said the driver had to talk to somebody, to break the monotony after driving all that time, for days on end.

The fourth time she said her husband was an ignorant brute.

The fifth time he said she was a bitch.

From then on they were to spend the rest of their lives fighting.

One day she said she was taking off, leaving everything behind. She was going back to her father's house.

Then the oldest son hugged her legs and said, "Don't do that, Mama."

"Oh, yes I will," she stroked his head. They were both crying. "You can come with me. I can't stand it any more."

"When we go over there, they're mean to us, there's so many other people."

"Grandpa likes you very much," she said. "He's not going to treat you mean."

"But there's the others. That great big bunch of people. It won't work. It's not the same thing."

The boy was eight years old. All of a sudden he stopped crying: "I know it won't be the same. It'll be worse."

"All right, I'll stay, but only on account of you." She too stopped crying and looked at her son, asking herself how the hell a little mite that size, a few years out of diapers, could know so much.

"I'll stay on account of you," she repeated.

"And for the others, Mama. There's five of us.

"Yes, and for the others."

"And on account of Papa."

"Yes, on account of your Papa, too."

Just then, the old man came out of the house onto the porch. He said: "As far as I'm concerned, you can go."

She began to cry again.

"No, Papa, Mama is staying on account of all of us," said the boy.

"The child has a sixth sense," he was to think on other occasions. "He must take after his mother. He probably even knows he wasn't born out of a woman's mouth, as I've tried to tell him." But at that moment he didn't think anything.

"I'm going out to the manioc patch," he announced, as if he no longer wanted to fight, as if he were a man of peace, as he was, always wanted to be.

"What for, Papa?" asked the boy.

"I'm going out to get a few dry stalks."

"What for, Papa?"

"Later you'll see."

They say that at the hour of death, a man sees his whole life clearly before his eyes, all that he has experienced since the day he was born. That was what the old man was thinking about, because he remembered everything, as if it were happening now.

Things seemed to gain a new meaning as he walked toward the manioc patch to get some stalks. His hard, rough heart had softened a little—and what he wanted to do was to draw close to his wife and apologize to her, ask her to stay. They already had five children and would have many more, like their great-great grandparents, their great-grandparents, their grandparents and their parents. God would help their children grow up strong and sound. God would give them many arms to help them work.

And it was his son who had caused him to feel that way.

A few days before, the boy had taken some dry manioc stalks out in the yard and, using sticks and pieces of wire, had fashioned a little gadget, something like a cage with a trap door, which the boy believed actually was a trap for birds. Proud and happy, he showed the invention to his father. "But I can't catch any canaries. They don't even come close," said the boy, pointing to the porch-post where the box hung, its useless mouth open, full of broken corn blowing away in the wind.

"I felt so sorry for him," the old man thought, recalling the smell of the new trap-door cage he had made, over-flowing with joy. He borrowed a canary, with which he caught another, a beautiful yellow one, a singer. The boy would spend the whole day lying in the hammock, swinging back and forth and looking at the canary. It was a happy time. Nobody fought any more. But real conversation, there in his house, was supplied only by the caged canary calling to the free birds that roosted on the ridgepole outside.

How many years ago had all that been? The old man plumbs his memory, but he can't manage to get the dates right. He vaguely remembers other things from that period, like conversations around the mouth of the furnace where they toasted the manioc flour, their faces lit by the glow of the burning logs. It was the year of the war that was going on all over the world. Although there were battles everywhere, they were all in distant places. There was some place called Japan, where the sun went after it had slid behind the mountain, distant but still visible from his porch late in the afternoon, at the hour of the Hail-Mary. It was there, in this Japan, that the world was coming to an end—this strange Japan where it was daytime when here it was night. It was his *compadre* Artur, the owner of the truck, who explained this to him. "I hope the civil war stays there, and doesn't come here," he said, throwing more wood into the furnace (that year nobody would be without manioc flour). Inside the shed the women and children were grating the manioc roots for the press, and a worker was stirring the flour so it would toast evenly. He was a worker with a light touch, there would be lots of fine flour, the best kind. "I hope so, too, *compadre*. But they're already saying the whole world is coming to an end. It seems this war will come to Brazil too and it'll be the worst one ever. God save us from a civil war, it's the most terrible kind."

He counted on his fingers by tens, each finger a decade, and calculated his age. He was sixty years old. At least he could never forget his birthday: New Year's Day, 1912. The years he had lived were neither many nor few. His father had reached ninety-odd; his father-in-law had lived past a hundred and even at that age had still gone riding around on a donkey, looking over his fields—because a doctor in Alagoinhas had forbidden him to ride horseback. The donkey being smaller, the fall would be shorter, if he fell. He never did. He died in bed.

"What kind of a world is this, where children don't respect their father, nor a wife her husband?" The old question stuck once more in his gullet. Would he die without an answer? Words that stuck in the throat went bad, like addled eggs that never hatched. There wasn't a man on earth who could explain this to him: why he experienced that brackish taste every time he thought about it. Twelve children he had brought into the world—for what? He loved them all so much, he longed for them one by one, every minute. And what did he get in return? Left behind. Alone.

No, he wouldn't look back, or he would see the desolate fields, the dried-up, useless heads of sisal that had brought his ruin. They might as well be gathered up into a bonfire and set alight. He could even have put them to the torch before leaving, just as he had wasted all he owned in the place, which hadn't even produced a rope to hang himself with. He must have been mad to do it—or had he been prompted by the Devil? His father-in-law, cautious but sharp, had warned him: "*Compadre*, this sisal is just a novelty, mark my words. It could lead plenty of folks to ruin." He could still hear the prudent words of advice he had not wanted to take—"Because a man's a fool if he just follows a whim, with nothing to back it up."

It happened that one time he planted tobacco, and it came out all right. That was a year of plenty. There was money left over to replaster and whitewash the whole house, which for years had scarred the landscape. Now a passer-by might raise his hat to the fortunate man who lived there, for he had even put in a little veranda and painted the door and windows blue. He pulled the old flagstones up from the floor and put down shiny new tiles, as in the wealthy farmers' houses; and he bought new clothes for himself, the wife and kids—two pieces each. That year they said tobacco, too, was just a craze—hard work for no profit. But he set his wife and youngsters to work hoeing and digging, tightened his belt, and the coffers began to fill. It seemed like a fortune that would never end. He thought he'd have the same luck with sisal, even though he had to hire a battalion of hands. He could hardly wait to see the truck piled high with the green fronds from his fields, setting off for the state factories over at Nova Soure. And when the machines churned out his palms transformed into lengths of cord stretching over leagues and leagues, to be taken in other trucks to the state capital, he'd be able to show his wife that it was the land, after all, that would ensure them a living, not the town. And that's how it would have been if he hadn't spent the bank loan before cutting the sisal. There they were, the immense cacti like swollen pineapple plants, pineapples that had gone wild and grown too much, waiting for the new owner to find workers for the harvest. It was all a question of money, he knew that. But his father-in-law had died and he didn't have anyone to endorse the refinancing papers from the bank. It was a disgrace, an insult. The men arrived, riding in a Volkswagen now instead of their jeep, with the bad news: it was time to pay the debt. "Give me a little more time, gentlemen... It's really tight just now."

They had no feeling, they didn't take into account that he was a man of his word, who would never fail to pay what he owed. They should have been a little more patient.

"The bank can't wait. If the money's due, it's due."

This all took place under the tamarind tree in the middle of town on market day. People saw and heard it all. The men told him they could refinance the loan, if he could find a new backer. Who? All his *compadres* were broke or being strangled by the bank with their own debts. He bowed his head, frowning, with an immense desire that a hole open up right under his feet so he could disappear into the ground, into the bottomless center of the earth. He thought about his brother, the only family he had left who owned anything. But his brother was right there taking it all in; if he had wanted to help he would already have offered. Then in the midst of the confusion a cry announced something nobody had expected, stirring up the crowd and increasing the fuss: "They're taking the master carpenter to jail! Come see, *Mestre*'s been arrested!"

No. He couldn't look to the side. He would see the face of shame, a shame he would never be able to forget.

"Brother, you see what's happening—these men have no patience. What shall I do?"

"The only way out is to sell the farm."

"Sell it? Just like that?"

"It's the only solution."

"But who'd buy it? Things like that take time."

"I'll buy it," said his brother.

"And if I don't want to sell?"

"The bank will take it over and sell it later on to someone else." His brother was looking at the men as if he was on their side.

"Then it's yours. Next Monday we'll settle our accounts." The old man was now addressing the bankers. "It's decided."

The same blood, the same flesh. Fruit of the same womb. Blessed is the fruit. A brother took away all he had and then patted him on the back as if he were doing him a favor. That day they came back together on this same road, talking. That is, the brother talked; he walked along in silence. There were only three words in his throat, nothing more: pride, greed, ingratitude. Three deadly sins together in a single person, there at his side. "Come on, name your price." The old man didn't hear the other's voice; he was thinking about distant things, maybe about an unbreakable order by which the universe was bound. God made earth, water and salt, sun and moon, animals and men—and the men were all brothers, and brothers of the same blood were the closest, because the same woman had suffered at their birth. "How much do you want for the farm?" The winds and the rain also have their maker, the same as the maker of men—Lord and Sovereign of Peace, Justice and Harmony, who would harm none of his creatures. "Come on, tell me. How much do you want?" That was when the old man spoke, as if returning to the real, treacherous world.

"Nothing," he said.

"Nothing what?"

"Nothing. I want nothing. Nothing."

"You joking, *compadre*?" said his brother.

"Nothing. I already said it and I'll repeat it as many times as you like. Nothing times nothing."

The next day he was calmer, and could listen to his brother's proposal, accept it, and assent to the deal. He was already paying interest on it—in regrets.

Much land, few signs.

Time proved that Antônio Conselheiro, the angel of destruction and death, knew what he was saying. Was it the end he was seeing before his eyes? Houses closed, farms abandoned. Now the true owner of everything was the scrub brush that grew wildly between the rows of cacti with their green palm leaves and dry tassels, for lack of hands to cut them down. Where were those hands? In buses, on top of trucks. Traveling south. South of Alagoinhas, south of Feira de Santana, south of Salvador, Itabuna and Ilheus, south of São Paulo, of Paraná, of Marilia, south of Londrina, going to the South of Brazil. Fortune was in the South, where they all went, where he was going. Once, in Feira de Santana, he had spent an entire morning at the bus station. It was like being in a great anthill, an endless bustle of people coming and going. He marveled: "If this place here is barely the beginning of the South, imagine what the rest is like!"

"The South ends in Paraguay," he was told by his wife's uncle, who had finally turned up in Junco for a visit after many years when no one knew if he was alive or dead.

"I know because I've been there. I know this whole world, inch for inch."

No one would guess that the man had once been a farmer. He talked knowingly, in a new adventurous style, letting everyone understand that behind each word was the unquestionable experience of a traveled man. He didn't tell things he had heard about, but rather what he had seen firsthand. He knew how to dress well, too; his everyday clothes were the kind that would be worn only once in a lifetime here, on your wedding day. And there was also the scar on top of his head, the dry hairless line that must have been made by a *machete*, witnessing to the accuracy of what he said. The scar resembled a groove in the side of a burned-off hill, and though it was carefully covered by a stylish felt hat, you could see it every time he scratched the sweat in his sparse hair. Yes, all he said was true. The man had left a piece of his flesh along the way; he had the style of someone who had known a world of different places. A man from Junco had already been as far as Paraguay. Nonsense. His son Nelo had probably gone much farther by this time. He must certainly know other routes, farther south than that, he—his son—who was much

68

younger and braver. It was impossible that the South should end in this place called Paraguay.

"And what is the land like, where you went, Sr. Caboco?"

"Very fine," said the man. "The problem is mosquitoes—they won't let a fellow sleep."

"What do they plant there in Paraguay?"

"Everything. But I didn't plant anything myself. My business was buying trinkets to sell in São Paulo."

"But Nego do Roseno, the owner of the notions shop, already does that right here."

"Except the things from there are worth a lot more money." The traveler took a little box out of his pocket, as though prepared to demonstrate to the old man that his doodads were not to be compared with those of some cheapjack corner-shop owner. He said the little box was called a ViewMaster, and was a little movie screen. The old man had thought it was field glasses.

"Look, this is São Paulo."

"Holy Virgin!" He had never seen such tall buildings, such a grand city. His first reaction was fear. All that masonry might fall down on a man's head. The traveler fiddled with the little box, changing the pictures.

Viaduto do Chá, Ibirapuera, Vale do Anhangabaú, the State Bank, Republic Square, Pacaembu.

Strange names, different. The people, the food, the weather—were they different too?

"It's very cold and you eat a lot. That's why I'm so fat."

In those climes there was nothing like the poverty of Junco, he continued. There were people everywhere and money to burn. In the beginning, he had worked as a bricklayer, and was invited to eat like this: "Clock's struck, chow's up."

"So can they even understand the way we talk, Sr. Caboco?"

"Some of 'em take a while, but they usually understand."

When talking about São Paulo, the man's mouth would water, and he would grow more important than ever. Down there, anyone could be bricklayer and boss-man at the same time, because at the end of the day you took a bath, put on fresh clothes, and nobody knew anything about anybody else.

"That's just fine, Sr. Caboco. All very pretty. But I'd never leave these good old parts here, no sir."

"If I were you, I'd give it a try. You're here all by yourself, in this place at the back of beyond. You should go down and join your son."

Don't even mention such a thing, he thought, remembering how silent and unfeeling his son was. He only sent money and only to his mother, and it seemed he had stopped sending it at that. And what about the messages? He paid no attention to them, as though a father wasn't worth a damn. But he couldn't help asking the question; the terrible love that he had for the boy came back to wound his heart.

"Have you seen him down there?"

"Well...it's been some time since I actually saw him."

It had been a good ten years since anyone turned up with news of his son. What was he like now? The old man didn't even have any pictures of him to keep and admire. He would never forget that cousin who arrived telling him, "Your son is a fine man. He never forgets he's from the

State of Bahia. I spent a night in his house and we slept in the same bed, head to foot, just like we used to do when we were kids." "How was it?" the old man would ask every time he met his cousin. It was a story that filled him with pleasure and pride.

"Is he well, Sr. Caboco? He must be rich as the devil."

The man hesitated. There seemed to be some bad feeling, some untold story or misunderstanding.

"Come on, tell me. I'm dying to know," the old man insisted. It wasn't possible that anyone could come from São Paulo and have nothing to say about Nelo, his son Nelo, the impulsive one who'd gone away against his father's wishes but made good, as people said in all the countryside hereabouts.

"Tell me everything, Sr. Caboco. It hurts every second you're silent."

"I only saw your son once. As I already told you, that was a long time ago."

Bad news? Sickness, death, poverty crossed his mind. Nobody concealed good things—people talked about them at once. Sr. Caboco shouldn't leave him in doubt.

"It was one time in São Miguel Paulista," the other began, calm and slow, measuring his words. "Actually, it was in a bar. Nelo was standing at the counter. He was overjoyed to see me." (The old man's eyes seemed brighter than before; they could have lit up a road. He was wondering if it would be as joyful on the day when they two, father and son, met. Whatever happened, he must live to see that day.) "But Nelo had already had too much to drink, he was slurring his words." The man called Caboco continued speaking calmly, without hurry, as if he hadn't much interest in the subject. He didn't want to insult his niece's husband, considered by all to be a good man. He was telling him; but what he said was an insult in itself. That was why he spoke very slowly. "Drink is the ruin of mankind, *Mestre*, I've always said it, and to see a man drunk is something that gives me no pleasure at all. Especially if the man is a relation of mine." That was true, the old man agreed. "But what about how happy Nelo was when he saw you, how was that again?" "Well, he had had too much to drink, like I said," continued the man called Caboco. "He made a big scene, yelling like crazy. 'Uncle!' he called to me. 'Tell this man here who our family is, back in Bahia.' This man was the owner of the bar, a mean-looking Portuguese who didn't talk much. 'Uncle!' Nelo yelled again, 'He won't sell me a glass of rum on credit. Isn't that an insult?' The owner of the bar didn't seem to be liking it much, and I saw trouble ahead. Not that I was afraid, mind you; when I was younger I got into my share of fights and I'm not sorry. So I paid for the rum Nelo wanted to drink on credit, because I'm not a man to leave a needy relation in difficulty, especially if he's far away from home. That was the only time I met him, *Mestre*. The ruin of man is drink, I repeat."

"You're right, Sr. Caboco. But a little drop now and then does nobody any harm—I have a little bottle of rum inside. Want to sample it?"

"God forbid," said the man. "I used to drink a lot. But now I don't touch the stuff. I joined the Seventh Day Adventists."

"Did you really, Sr. Caboco? That's a new one on me."

Later the old man thought: If I had known that, I wouldn't have wasted my time talking to him. Those Pro-

testants are beyond the laws of God. That man was tempted by the Devil, I don't know why I didn't suspect it at
once. As far as I'm concerned, Protestants and Communists
are all the same.

Flour out of the same sack, Protestants, Communists
and members of the National Union of Democrats—that's
what Uncle Ascendino would have said. The last saint left
on earth, if he were still alive. Eternal memories of that
silver head, always protected from the weather by a white
cap that could have belonged to an educated man of affairs.
He died as he lived: praying. The soul of a singing bird,
the heart of a child. He left this world like a saint, virgin
and immaculate. He had marvellous hands—hands that
could make three-cornered shelves, candlesticks, cabinets
for holy images and braids in the little girls' hair. Now he
was giving joy to the children in Paradise, while here below
everything was in ruins. "If longing could kill, dear old
Dino, I would already be up there beside you, joining in
the chorus of your prayers along with all the angels. Is it
green in heaven, Ascendino? Is there plenty of rain?"

Memories, battles, hopes.

"All U.D.N. people are dishonest. All U.D.N. people end up in the lowest depths of hell." Uncle Ascendino
wouldn't go into the house of someone who had a picture
of Juracy Magalhães on the wall, wouldn't accept work or
coffee from anyone who followed that leering villain. Communists are not to be trusted, they're always laughing. And
laughter is a sinner's habit. All you had to do was look at
Juracy's teeth in the photograph, his false face, his impious
grin, to see he was dishonest. He would be the downfall
of the country. He was a threat to Christian people, aided

by a gang who only pretended to believe in God. But the Almighty knew which side the faithful were on, and which side the sinners. "Vote for the Social Democrats!" Uncle Ascendino would yell as he passed a house, and then walk on, chanting his blessings and Hail-Marys. The heavens would surely defend the earth from those infidels.

Heaven is full of flowers. The flowers of the month of May, Holy Mary's month. After death, life is a perpetual month of May. Heavenly blossoms: roses, white lilies and jasmine. All the flowers that ever were, blooming. There's no such thing as drought up there. Lizards and field mice scampered to hide in the underbrush at his slow passing. The old man prayed. Now he heard something else besides his own footfalls. He heard his voice:

*In heaven, in heaven,*
*With my Mother I shall be,*
*In heaven, in heaven,*
*We shall sing in harmony.*

"Nelo, Noemia, Judite, Gesito, Tonho, Adelaide—" again he called to his children there on the road, as if suddenly time had rolled back, and it wasn't almost noon (the sun was already very high) but daybreak, and as though he were awakening to the happy celebration of the roosters and birds surrounding the dark, quiet house. He was always the first to wake up. And before rising, he would stop a few seconds to listen to his children's breathing. Many times he would wait a while to call them, because he was sorry to disturb their rest. The sleep of early morning is the best of all, the most enjoyable. "Nelo, Noemia, Judite, Gesito, Tonho, Adelaide—"he called again, because the first time he didn't hear an answer; they were taking a long time to get up. "Wake up, come on. Come and say prayers."

*Kyrie, eleison,*
*Christe, eleison.*
*Kyrie, eleison.*

Impossible. What was the matter with these children today?

The dog answered him. Whining desperately, it was running after him so fast it scattered dust onto the brush beside the fenceposts. "Go home!" The old man threw a stone, which whizzed between the dog's ears. The dog ducked its head, seeming to get the point. But it didn't go back. Now it walked slowly: it was near its master, smelling his smell. It still whined as though crying, a lament he could almost understand. "Go back to your new owner," said the old man, picking up a stick in his hand. Rearing up on its hind feet, the dog shook its head and front paws, as though about to embrace him. "Just like a person," he thought. "He's almost talking. All right, if you want to come, come on then," he told the dog, throwing the stick down. "But you'll have twice the distance to go. The trouble of coming and then of going back again. They told me I wasn't supposed to bring a dog." He could have said: Look at the irony of it. The creature I want to be rid of won't leave me. You could even say he's the one who turned out to be my best child.

And so it was that he came to the village and went inside the general store: without a penny and accompanied by a tired dog slavering at the mouth.

"Did I take too long?"

"You're early, *Mestre*. We're still loading up down at the tannery," said the truck driver.

"Then I'll buy us a round."

He had eaten nothing. The invitations to lunch from

his *compadre* Artur couldn't tempt him: he had no desire to eat, or to do anything. He went around the empty square, knocking on each door in turn and shouting: "I'm leaving, friends. I came to say good-bye." The majority of these houses belonged to farmers who lived in remote places and came here only on Mass days or for holy pilgrimages. The square. Quiet, calm, lazy as always. A church and a crossroads, nothing more. Pretty soon it would be animated by the snorting of a truck; a few faces would watch through the windows, lamenting the departure of whoever was leaving, wanting to go too. At night, after the lights were turned out, the werewolves and headless mules would appear: ghosts would stalk. The cities were illuminated, full of life—they had no ghosts.

"When're we going to have a real bash again, *Mestre?*"

"That's all over," he said with a chuckle (the rum had perked him up). "But if you can find an accordion player and some girls, we'll dance until the truck leaves."

He had been married in that church, and there all his children and everyone else's had been baptized. He must have more than a hundred *compadres*, friends whose sons and daughters were his godchildren.

Nothing could ever be the way it was before. This square could never be like the dense undergrowth that the *vaqueiros* (sons and grandsons of João da Cruz) had found and tamed. ("No, *Mestre*, it was the cattle. The cattle came looking for water, and there was a lake down yonder. The men came following the sound of the cowbells.") Yes. But it was a Cruz who first built a house, the chapel and the crossroads. The place couldn't be called Dove Lake or Spotted Rock nowadays: there was no more lake, nor spot, nor the famous rock. Now it was just a square. To look back was to waste time.

The old man drank, chatted, sang, danced. He told and retold all the stories of the past. The truck pulled up at the door of the general store exactly as the church bell struck the six chimes of the Hail-Mary hour. He crossed himself, taking off his hat; then he jumped up on the truck bed.

"Come on in the cab with me, *Mestre*, it's a lot softer," invited the driver.

"No, thanks. I like it better out here where I can see the scenery."

"Up in the cab's more comfortable. C'mon."

"No, you might meet a nice-looking girl along the road, you never know."

"What about the dog, *Mestre*? Is it going or staying?"

It was true. What about the dog? The poor animal was once again pawing and whining.

"Hand him up here, kid, I'm taking him."

He would take the dog that his wife didn't want to Feira de Santana. She could go to hell.

Old sad faces appeared for the last time; arms were raised in farewell, probably the last one.

"God go with you." The voices trailed after him, clinging, dying away behind.

"I'm leaving, friends. Ha, Ha!" He raised his arm and slapped the cab of the truck with the palm of his hand. "Git up, old horse." He began to sing,

*Hello, New World,*
*Good-bye my lady fair,*
*I'm off to Feira de Santana*
*I'll sell my cattle there.*

The horn honked gaily as the truck went slowly

downhill. They passed through the alleyway behind the market place, gained the street at the bottom of town and then turned onto the dusty road to Serrinha. But the old man's voice was stronger than the horn. It echoed above the houses, filled the square. Then it faded in the dust, in the direction of the sun, which was also disappearing.

"Ha, Ha!" he shouted down the narrow road, ducking the tree branches that whipped past him. "Whoooooooo, Boy!"

# PART THREE

## The Land Maddens Me

# I

"WHO AM I?"

Ask him, don't ask me. I know who you are, madam. There's no doubt in my mind who you are. I can even recognize you in the darkness of this little room, where we meet and stare at each other, our opposed forms barely defined by the weak light that comes from the hallway. This room was once called the "visitors' parlor," remember? Yes, you remember. Now you are the only visitor, but you don't count. I know you didn't come here of your own free will. We all dread an evil hour like this one, even in our dreams; and so you spent your life wearing out the beads on your old black rosary. In each prayer was a request: eternal life for your children, eternal salvation for yourself. In each bead a small fragment of your own sorrows. Do you see now? Everything comes to an end. We are born, we grow up and our lives are finished. What is left? Longings. This is how we see each other: quiet, calm, concealed by a multitude of commandments that keep us from saying what we are.

"All's well, praise God," that's all we can say, lowering our eyes or shifting them to one side. We've stopped communicating, we don't say what we feel, we don't look each other in the eye. Now I'm the one who is asking why. Listen: your husband is sawing boards and pounding nails in the kitchen, to make a coffin. Maybe he will bury himself in the coffin with the dead man, although he will spend the rest of his days pretending to be alive. The work will take him all night. He will not need our help or the help of a lantern; tonight nobody will have the nerve to turn off the electric generator. We are scared of our own shadows, which drag after us in the faint light of these same light bulbs. They are low-wattage bulbs; even in light we are poor. But don't worry yourself overmuch; it's not good for you. There is always the possibility of forgetting, the hope of things returning to the way they were before. Listen again. Your man (perhaps you loved him once, perhaps not even that) clears his throat. He must be talking to the saw or the hammer. He says nothing to us, nor is anything necessary. Don't ask me anything—that's not necessary either.

"The dead don't talk," she would answer me, and rightly so.

I had just discovered something: we were the same size, she and I, body pressed to body. Like two sweethearts who meet again after a long absence and, having held each other in a long and passionate embrace, keep squeezing and patting each other. For the first time I wanted to embrace her; but I couldn't, because she was squeezing my neck with all the strength she had left in her dry, calloused hands—hands that had known a lifetime of washing plates and pans, sweeping houses and yards, trimming children's hair, cutting and patching the scraps with which she dressed us, washing dirty clothes. God's love has not yet brought her recompense; maybe she doubts that this love will ever come.

"Do you remember me? Who am I?"

I was going to say, "You are the oldest daughter of that man looking down from the wall. And you're the mother of the other one stretched out on the floor over there, asleep forever." I wanted to talk, but I couldn't. As long as her hands cut off my breath, I wouldn't be able to tell her anything. I felt the hour of my death had come; yet I was only twenty years old, and still had a whole life ahead of me.

The only thing that occurred to me was a simple question: "Why are you trying to kill me?"

If I could, I would have added, "Don't let me die without understanding this."

We never loved each other, that's the answer to everything. And I was asking myself why.

"Why are you choking me?"

It was as if she were spanking me again and telling me to behave, repeating: "Some are born good, others bad."

It was as if I were saying to her once more: "I didn't ask to be born at all."

It wasn't always so bad, praise God. She used to cut my hair, my fingernails and toenails. She used to wash my feet. She even used to pick lice out of my hair. It was she who gave me a bath from the basin with a tin dipper.

The same woman who was now trying to strangle me.

I know that face.

I've seen it crazy before. This isn't the first time.

I recognize these hands.

They once pushed me out the door, when the old man sold the farm and I asked for my share. The farm had belonged to us, I reasoned, and "us" means "me too." They wouldn't give me anything and I said, "Someday

I'll come back and kill you all!'' I was excommunicated. I never went back and I never killed anybody, but I'm still banished.

In those eyes I see again ancient pathways, torches, crosses, spells. And I find myself at the nearest crossroads, with seven stakes in my hand.

So I will say her name, although it is hard for me to do so.

It is more of a gesture, actually. Something you say just to be talking. Let go of my throat. Let me find words again. Please. (It was as if she had heard me and understood. Because at that moment her hands relaxed and slowly let go of my neck. I recovered my breath, became aware of my own breathing: I was still alive.)

"You're my mother," I say, certain I was expressing an unquestionable truth.

"No!" she said, and her voice made the rafters, beams and rooftiles shudder. As she shouted, her hands were already squeezing my neck again.

"I am the Archangel Raphael," she added, her eyes turning upward, as though to confirm that she was no longer of this world.

I nodded to show that I agreed: "Yes, you're the Archangel Raphael," I said as soon as she took her hands away once and for all.

"Now you know. Everyone must know." Her words were accompanied by a strange sort of bark.

I thought: Nelo won't be able to sleep, with all this noise.

He was still there on the floor, right beside us.

# II

(That night I had two jobs: attending the wake of a dead man and taking my mother to the hospital in Alagoinhas, the closest town that had one. It was not far. Only thirty leagues' journey. Fifteen going, fifteen coming back.)

# III

But first, let's listen to a crazy old man, crazy as a coot, crazy as a loon, crazy as anything you like.

"In this land, the living can't sleep and the dead can't rest in peace," said Alcino in the quiet of the night. Once again he spreads his wings over us like a vulture descending onto a carcass. Later it was known that no one heard a single word that he spoke through his foul beak of a mouth. Not even those who were two steps away from him, sitting on the sidewalk with their backs to the church and their faces to the moon.

Benevolent full moon.

Roosters crow outside their time. Listen. Drunks and dogs whine. The night itself is in pain. These laments come from the place we are heading for, says the crazy man. Hell is big, there's room for us all. Up above, inside the moon, Saint George hears, sees and knows all, but says nothing. Here below men divine signs of rain in the shining wells.

"My name is Aleixo. Crooked I come, crooked I go," says Alcino. It's as if he were saying, "My name is Lo-o-oneliness."

Alcino was right: nobody wanted to sleep. Nor to eat, to love or to hate their sad, tired wives of every night. Yet he was addressing the air, and not people like the mayor, the police officer, the druggist, relatives and hangers-on, field hands come from far away, stumbling and discouraged: "A man who hangs himself can't have a church funeral."

Half-man, half-flame is Alcino, with his burning zeal. Earthly and palpable, inhuman and volatile. This was his greatest day—when all would witness the turmoil and the martyrdom of one assumed to be only a village idiot, yet who saw himself as the guide appointed to lead sinners down the road toward an eternity without suffering, his croaking voice like that of a haunted raven. "Sinners, one more of you has gone to hell" —all day long his cry raised the dust in the square, echoed through the back streets, under beds, behind stoves.

"Husband, make that crazy man shut his mouth."

"How, woman?"

"I can't bear to hear it any more."

"Then put your fingers in your ears."

From the sidewalk in front of the church he runs toward the door of the general store. He stops and shouts. From the general store he runs down into the back streets. The bell tolls and he runs, runs, runs. Always at a gallop, like a horse. He was running and yelling when he came on someone he never expected to meet again in his life. He prayed for legs to flee, they weren't there. He screamed for help, nobody heard him. And as he fell to the ground in a faint, he was grabbed, shaken, revived by a familiar voice: "Don't be afraid, man, a dead person can't harm anybody."

"People who talk too much break their teeth"—Alcino was sorry for all he had said a little while ago. "Hit me, punish me, hurt me." To himself he thought, my hour has come. Death is here to get me. "For the love of God, let me live."

"Don't crawl, man, you're not a rat," said the other sternly, like a father.

"I don't want to die." Alcino still couldn't stand up by himself. He leaned on the other's arms, which were not cold as he expected a dead man's arms to be.

"What the hell difference does it make?"

"You've come to settle a score between us," said Alcino, thinking, this particular sinner hasn't gone to hell yet.

"Come on, Alcino old man," the other's voice was sympathetic, paternal—"you know we're brothers. And between brothers differences don't exist. Or rather, they do exist but they pass away."

As though he were just waking up, and standing now on his own two feet, Alcino said.

"I never knew we were brothers."

The other man put a hand on his shoulder. The hand was not cold either.

"Look at it like this. You're my friend. And friends are like brothers."

"That's true." Alcino was showing a new interest now. Little by little, he was losing his fear.

"What's more, you're a Cruz."

"Alcino Cruz, at your service."

"So, then," the other explained things patiently, like a schoolteacher. "You're a Cruz and so am I. That means we're part of the same family. And if we're from the same family, it's as if we were brothers."

One thing he knows for sure, and that's how to talk

pretty, thought Alcino. Then he said, "That's how it should be, but that's not how it is."

The other raised his voice a little, thinking, what a stubborn bastard. "You don't have to believe me, believe God."

"What I believe is that our relatives are our worst enemies." Alcino scratched his head, unhappily.

"I'm talking about us two, man."

Alcino sighed, greatly relieved.

"Ah, well then. That's the most important thing you've said."

If he could, he would keep this instant of joy forever. Did he really have a brother in this world after all? A friend-brother? Yes sir.

"Well, then, brother," said his companion, "the thing is, I need a favor from you."

Once a brother, always a brother. In life and in death. He would even go to hell if necessary.

"Name it."

Their meeting was taking place in the humblest part of this humble village. Walls and dunghills, turds and garbage, provided the setting for such important revelations. Anyone else coming from São Paulo, even if he had spent only one day there, would have said, "What filth, what shit!" This one was different, he didn't complain about these things. One more point in his favor, in Alcino's opinion.

"I need a little help from you to jump over that wall there. I've already tried several times, before you got here, but I couldn't do it."

"Be careful, brother. That wall is the sergeant's. He's mean as a dog."

"I know, Alcino. But the problem is I left a treasure inside there."

"Buried coins?" The crazy man's eyes lighted up. If it was enchanted gold, could it be for him?

"Better than that. Much better," the other assured him, licking his lips as though he had just had a bite of something very tasty. I've stood up to every challenge in my life so far. I can't go to the grave without facing this last one."

"It was because of some enchanted coins given to me by a dead soul that I went crazy. I went crazy because I couldn't manage to dig up the money." Alcino hadn't paid attention to the second part of the conversation. He thought it was really money they were after in the sergeant's yard.

"The only thing worse than the struggle for money is women—right, brother? Women are our downfall."

Women? The only females he knew anything about were the she-donkeys: Alcino could talk about them. He knew all their habits, whims and vices. His problem wasn't caused by females, either two-legged or four-legged, but by greed and avarice. The dead soul had said, "Take along pious Theodora, she knows all the prayers." It was to be like this: Theodora would pray as he dug until he found the money, which was inside a cement box lined with gold. It was the treasure of Jesuit priests from olden times, rich, miserly people, whose souls still walk the earth in suffering. Alcino didn't take Theodora along, he wanted all the money for himself. He dug all night. When he found the cement box, he threw himself on it in greedy haste, trying to lift the lid. He was just getting it open when a gang of bandits from hell arrived to ruin everything. If the religious lady had been there praying, the bandits wouldn't have dared come. The next morning Alcino went back to the place. There was no trace of the hole he had dug, as if nobody had ever disturbed the soil there.

"Come on." Once you've gone crazy, thought Alcino, you're never scared of anything again. The other put his foot on Alcino's interlaced hands and tried to raise himself up over the wall. "As heavy as this, he'll never get up to heaven," thought Alcino bitterly. It was true: no matter how hard they tried, his friend (a true brother) always slipped back down and had to start all over again. After many long efforts, they gave up, worn out. "A weight like that will break St. Michael's scales," Alcino thought again, still more bitterly.

They sat down at the foot of the wall to rest. They meditated: one, on the best way to get into the sergeant's back yard, the other, on the treasure inside.

"If we had a little something to drink, we could do it."

"You're right," said the other, encouraged. "But where're we going to get a drink?"

"At a brothel."

"What the hell's that? Some new kind of store?"

"Come on, Alcino. Haven't you ever been to a whorehouse?"

"You're dreaming, brother. This isn't São Paulo."

"It's true, there's no brothel here." (He thought a little.) "What if we opened one? After all, the place is getting quite advanced. It ought to have a whorehouse."

"Brother!" Alcino gave a little leap. "That's an idea." He sat down again, pensive. "But where will we find the whores?"

"That's what I was worrying about. None of the women around here will want to."

"To this day there has only been one, ever since I was old enough to understand anything," Alcino informed him. "She died at it."

"Syphilis?"

"You don't have to believe me, believe God. But she really did die screwing. It was when the Petrobrás people were around here. During the day the men tramped through the woods, and at night they formed a line outside her door. They finished her off, poor thing. She died moaning."

"We'd better have a drop of rum, Alcino. Let's forget the subject."

The crazy man said nothing. He went back to meditating.

"What's the matter, friend? Something wrong?"

"The problem is, I don't have any money."

"Neither do I," said the other, considering the situation.

"Don't lose hope. There's always a way around everything."

"The only thing there's no way around is death," said Alcino with unexpected wisdom.

"And so," the other continued in a philosophical vein, "buying on credit is the solution if you want a drink and you're a little hard up."

Listen, sinners. Hear me, you miserable beggars. I've yet to meet a man more intelligent than this brother of mine. But Alcino's pride was short-lived.

"The worst of it is, nobody will sell anything on credit to a looney," he said.

The other poked at the ground with a piece of stick.

"Nor to a dead man either."

"That's why I wait every night for a wandering soul to offer me enchanted money." Alcino's dreamy eyes gazed into the distance, in the direction of the cemetery.

"You had your chance," declared the other. "Why did you throw it away?"

"Greed and covetousness, like I told you."

"You'll have a long wait," thought his companion. Aloud: "I know what we can do!" he exclaimed, giving Alcino a tap on the leg. "Run over to the general store and tell them Papa sent you to get a bottle of rum. Have them put it on his bill."

"That's it! They'll believe that. Your father got here just a while ago to make your coffin. Everybody knows that, and they know the old man likes his rum." Alcino jumped three times for joy. He took off, then stopped, looked back and called, "Brother, can I call your father Papa?"

"Are we brothers or aren't we?" said the other.

Sometimes it almost seems that men can fly, if they really need to. Quick as a wink, it seemed, Alcino had gone on his errand and returned, with the sad news:

"Brother, brother, they won't believe me. They're sons-of-bitches, all of them. Brother, brother"—the harsh raven's cry filled the air, further disturbing the sleep of those already half-awake. "Brother, brother!"

There was no one and nothing there. "He must be screwing the sergeant's wife. Give it to her, brother," he thought, climbing up onto the wall. There wasn't even a shadow inside the yard. He cried out again, "Brother, brother," and climbing down off the wall, he continued to run and shout. He turned down the alley, flew up the hill that gave onto the square and, quick as lightning, reached the sidewalk in front of the church, where he intended to put things to rights. He was going to preach the finest sermon of his life. It started like this:

"Come, and I will shelter you."

Mad Alcino was talking to the air. He seemed to want to drive the whole world mad.

"I am your land. I am your father and your mother."

# I V

He was squatting on the ground beneath the stars, and wondered at how many there were of them: the Southern Cross, St. James's Way, and many others whose names he could no longer remember. He continued looking up for some time, still with his pants down, forcing himself to do what he had come to do. He no longer needed to. It was uncomfortable, keeping his legs apart—but all these gymnastics were for nothing. He began to feel indignant.

If he looked ahead of him he would see a black shadow, the shape of a man squatting down. He would not recognize himself in that shape. He refused to use the toilet, it was so dirty. They had left a lantern in the doorway, and it was the light from this lantern that projected his shadow. The lights in the street had been turned off a long time ago, it must be very late. He got up, adjusting his trousers. The back of the house faced a dark patch of tall grass full of strange noises. He walked faster. He was afraid.

Back in bed, he felt his guts rumble again. It was the water, it was the food, it was everything. He opened the bedroom window and sat on the sill. When he really had to go, he would jump out onto the sidewalk and take a few steps into the street, which was also very dark. The light from the lantern now stretched his shadow long across the level floor, far away. He went back to bed, asking God to let daybreak come soon, make the clock hurry, have pity. It was his turn to discover that here the nights are slower than the days.

Everything now was a great, impatient longing. Let them say what they would, that town life was better. "Come back, come back, dressed in white and with a ribbon in your hair, come back, with stars in your eyes. Come back to my arms, with a child on either side."

A confusion of desires, regrets, and doubts. Worn by the years, ravaged by alcohol, he could no longer see a way of making a new start. He had had a wife and children, just as he had also once had a job and a clean toilet. And a bad temper. Hers was stubborn too—it was mule against mule. Even so he would still be capable of kneeling at her feet, come back, come back. He wanted a chance for love to be reborn.

An old man coughs and groans. After the groan, the gagging, lack of air. He remembered when he was a boy. He used to make balloons out of inflated cow bladders. Then he would pop the balloons by kicking them. The old man who was coughing might pop, too, by the sound of it. His grandfather used to cough and say, "The father sold the farm to go along with what his woman wanted. The son is a weakling just like his father."

Still coughing, his grandfather would call to someone, nobody knew whom. Then he would get up, take a lantern, and go out to the privy.

"*Padrinho,* use the chamberpot. Don't go out in the rain."

He wouldn't answer. He would keep on walking stiff

and straight, without leaning on anyone. Dignity. But he never thought about putting a toilet inside the house; he made the outhouse separate from the house proper. He died complaining about other people's weakness. And now he comes back after all these years to haunt me, to complain about mine.

Outside, as he looked up at the stars, he thought of his father. Something that had to do with the evening dew. An old bit of advice about the weather, which he had never forgotten.

"Don't go around with your head uncovered. Wear your hat. People who go around with their heads exposed to the weather lose their senses. Hats were invented in the time of Our Lord to cover men's heads. And every man should wear a hat. You have yours. I gave you one so you wouldn't go around with your head uncovered."

Almost every night he dreamed about his father telling him to wear his hat. He saw him chew his words, the same way his mother liked to chew a twist of tobacco. He would wake up and be unable to get back to sleep again. He would think and think. He would reflect that he had gone about bareheaded all his life because, when he left home, he had forgotten to take his hat.

New voices filled the house. Children fighting. Children shouting. Children, children. And the mothers, who never got along, perhaps because they were sisters. The bell rang out, swinging back and forth, calling people to Mass. His grandfather's voice demanding peace and quiet. Everyone obeyed him. The house was happy again.

He had all this recorded, photographed. All the faces, all the voices.

Things gone by.

There was only one brother left, who snored and mumbled as he slept in the next room. The last tooth to be pulled. A brother who hadn't kept the old straw hat his father bought him on market day to keep him from going around with his head exposed to the weather.

The time came when he put a hoe over his shoulder and walked to the fields. It was a very long walk, which became shorter as he grew bigger.

Later it was the walk to school, beyond the farm entrance gate. The road seemed endless until it gradually became a simple path, for each day he woke up a little taller, seeing things shorter. Only the sun continued very high, rising in the east and setting in the west, but it was never the same sun. It was born and died to be born again, so it wasn't the same sun.

And the sun dried up everything, sapping the hearts of men, parching their flesh, as it seemed, to the bone, drying them until they disappeared—and time went on, peaceful and primitive, monotonous as an old village square that tries hard not to decay, as if decay were not inevitable; as if, after one day was over, another wouldn't come sharp-toothed to take another bite out of our lives, leaving the beginnings of our death behind with each mouthful. And this is the worst drought of all, the worst journey of all.

He thought, in order to distract himself. He thought, to make sleep come.

We were born in a harsh land, where everything was already condemned from the beginning. Harsh sun. Harsh rain. The sun burns into our brains and the rain washes away the fences, leaving only the barbed wire, so that the men had to replace the fenceposts and staple up the same barbed wire. And as soon as they finish making the fence, they have to root out all the weeds, the strangling, spreading vegetation that has sprung up with the rain for which they prayed so hard to God.

He repeated all this to me in the morning. And he also said:

"That's why I don't know if I'm going back or staying. I think it doesn't make any difference now. Because the time and the weather that have worn out my straw hat are now eating up the place I left behind in São Paulo. Do you understand that, Totonhim? Did I answer your question right?"

## V

My son Nelo sent word:

She hits herself against the wall. I never thought she could still be so strong. It's the moon, the full moon. The wall trembles. Pretty soon the house will fall down. Pretty soon I'll be buried under the tiles. What can I do?

"Her. Her. Her."

"Who, Papa?"

"Her. The boss-woman. Your mother."

"She broke the bottle I had put away in the bedroom. It was for the workers. One more disgrace I'll have to pay for." Disgrace. Everything for him is a disgrace, a failure. I think of telling him:

"What you call disgrace is just things falling apart." He wouldn't understand. Nor would anything change, even if he did. The men (there were two) were working on the building across the street, with their helpers. It began to rain.

"*Mestre*, it's time to warm up a little. We're sopping wet."

They must have heard everything: the front door was open.

Papa crossed the living room, the shards of glass in his hands. He went out into the muddy yard. He was going to throw the glass where nobody would get cut. This house is always full of children.

"Whore. Impudent whore."

"Better if I were! Better to be a whore than to be married to a fool like you."

The children complained, "Mama, leave the fight for afterwards. We're late."

She went back to ironing the children's school uniforms, muttering to herself.

"For heaven's sake, Mama, are you going to start again?" I say.

"You're always on his side. It's because you don't live here to see what goes on."

"Papa's working. He's not drinking."

"Working, hah! He's working on his rum bottle."

He goes into the kitchen looking for food. He doesn't find any; it's all been eaten. He takes out an egg and fries it, throws manioc flour on top of the egg and carries the skillet out to the back porch. The children have already rushed off to school. I turn up the volume on my radio. I don't want the neighbors to hear us. Yesterday it was the same thing. My littlest brother said to me, "You know what? I'm never going to get married." I laughed. It was funny to hear that coming from a little kid.

I go into the bedroom and get my clothes together. I'm going back home. Home? I'm going back to Junco.

Better to be alone than... Honor your father and mother? I had been planning to spend two weeks with them. Two days were enough. Placing one foot in front of the other, like someone walking on eggs, Mama goes across the kitchen and stands in the doorway to the porch. She doesn't move. She looks over his shoulders. His back to her, Papa doesn't realize that anyone is watching him eat. He becomes aware of it only when he goes to get a glass of water. He says something that I don't hear. What I do hear shortly is the thump of a body falling to the floor. And the screams. The *screams*. I run. She is already getting up.

"I punched her. Look what she did to me." Papa shows me the toothmarks on his arm. A house slipper flies through the air and lands on his face. She runs out into the street. Papa flies after her. I follow them.

His dream was to have all his children together under the same roof. He told me that once. It was an appeal: be patient with your mother. She's not reasoning too well.

Now it's I who tell him, Be patient.

The words come out as if they weren't being said by me. They must belong to somebody else—perhaps an angel. Perhaps.

"Are you two going to spend the rest of your lives like this? Two old people, good heavens."

He wasn't listening, nor did he see me, or feel my hand on his arm.

Mama had vanished from our sight. We were going back. At all the windows were staring faces. I spoke softly, slowly, calmly. That strange calm that once or twice has come to me, exactly at times of greatest despair.

"It's time you found a way of getting along." I almost said, "A decent way to live." It would be the same thing as talking about rope to somebody who doesn't want to hang himself, or can't for lack of strength.

"She ran off, but she'll be back. I'll kill her."

"Papa, it's better for you two to separate. It's better than..."

"I'll kill her, I swear I'll kill her. There's no other way. She ought to be killed."

He'll kill her, and then kill himself. What I always feared and now wished for. Honor your father and mother? Tonight will be another night when I won't be able to sleep. I'll think about the children. Who will take care of them? There are only three. But who would stay with them? "The main thing," said one of my sisters, "is that we're all very close, us kids." I answered her, "It's because none of us has any money." She corrected me, "Nelo did." Yes, it was true. But he lived so far away.

"Can I ask you a favor?"

"What is it?"

"Stop drinking."

"Your mother's been giving you an earful, hasn't she? Oh, my God in Heaven!"

"You've started drinking again, haven't you, Papa?"

"I never missed work because of drink, I never ruined my chances, or wasted my money on it. Now, she..."

And, once again, the fateful word:

"I'll kill her. She won't live to see tomorrow."

We've reached the building site. I'm dripping wet now. And what's worse, I feel like having a few drinks, too. I almost say so, I almost invite him: since there's nothing else to do...

He tells the men to come down from the scaffolding. "Nobody works any more today. No more work."

He always talked that way, repeating what he said. The children think he's odd. And I was beginning to think that things were far worse than that. Honor your father and mother? If you think too much you lose your sleep, and that's one step away from losing your mind.

"Now you see what it's like. You have to live here to know," he told me, going with the two men toward the bar on the corner. I knew what they were going to do. Only I didn't know what *he* might do once he was falling-down drunk.

There aren't just three. We were twelve children. What will happen to those twelve, without the two of them?

I went back by the same route, following in Mama's steps. I was going to take her away with me for a few days. It was all I could do.

My son Nelo sent word to me:

Now she has stopped beating the wall, and is stretched out on the floor. She seems to be accepting things.

From here to Inhambupe it's seven leagues São Paulo has thirty leagues of paved streets I never got lost there Nelo my son I got a letter from him yesterday—

I took my son Nelo to Inhambupe to fulfill a promise we went in my father's oxcart my son Nelo went for a walk through the streets and got lost I found him near the gas pump at the Hotel Rex I gave him a whipping three times seven is twenty-one São Paulo is more than three times the distance from here to Inhambupe my son Nelo never got lost—

My son Nelo has been sending me money for twenty years he supports me I never was so ashamed and so afraid as I was that day in Inhambupe my son Nelo wrote to say—

Give your father some good advice Nelo, my son, your

father actually took poison this man is my greatest burden—

"No, Mama. It wasn't him, it was Uncle."

Your brothers are all on his side Nelo my son only you stood by me—

"I remember, Mama. I was a little kid. But I remember."

He's always saying that a man should be able to talk to God Nelo my son look here, is that the kind of thing a sensible man should say—

I can smell the flowers there used to be in the old days: roses. Roses of all colors, of all scents. The oily scent of a candle burning in the niche. The scent of my cousin Zoia's body. The sweaty smell of the men coming in from the fields. Tonight all of this will die forever.

Nelo my son your father became moonstruck after he took poison from here to Inhambupe the same distance as the streets in Salvador São Paulo has thirty leagues of streets send for me—

I don't know where she got that idea, I say, Papa never drank poison. It was his brother, but it was a long time ago. People of the same stripe, she must be thinking. One imitates what the other does. Rum.

Tell me Nelo my son what kind of a life is this, for a wife to be taking beatings from her husband send for me—

He was in the house in town, on his deathbed. He was in the room with the images of saints. His wife and children were crying. One son, eight daughters. My uncle had no luck.

"Why aren't you crying, Papa?"

"I wish I could," he said, lowering his eyes, I think he was ashamed. "A person who cries suffers everything right away and then the suffering passes. A person who doesn't cry keeps all the suffering bottled up in his throat."

Smell of death, color of death. My uncle's face looked like the face of a frog.

"Papa will be born again," said Zoia.

A Mass said every year for Our Lady of Amparo. A pilgrimage every year to the shrine of Our Lady of Candeias. A visit to Our Lord of Bonfim, in Bahia. A cross placed on top of the hill behind the house. These penances saved my uncle.

I pinched Zoia's fuzzy leg.

"I want to come too."

"Where, little boy?"

"I want to come with you."

"Keep quiet and cry, little pest."

Nelo my son have compassion on your mother your poor mother come and—

*Pardon us, Lord,*
*Have pity on us.*
*Pardon us, Lord,*
*For our sins.*

The holy-water in the cup from which he had drunk the poison. The crucifix at the head of the bed. The picture of the Sacred Heart of Jesus in his hand.

"Kneel down, lad."

*Better to die*
*Better to die*
*Than to offend You.*

"I want to go to Candeias. I've never been."

"Be quiet and pray."

"But you're not praying."

"I'm crying."

I can't stand it any more I won't I can't Nelo my son

this is no life come.

Papa made the cross. He painted it blue. The priest blessed it. The procession left from our house and walked to my uncle's house. He, my uncle, dragged the cross on his shoulders, alone. From time to time he stopped to rest. I closed my eyes so as not to see the blood running down from his torn shoulders. We sang sacred songs. On the ribbon was printed: Remembrance of Our Lord of Bonfim, Salvador, Bahia. We ordered (I should say, Papa ordered) a Mass to be celebrated at the foot of the cross. God saved my uncle.

"What was it that he had, Mama?"

"Temptations. A person only does such things when he is tempted by the Devil."

Nelo my son the aim of these ill-traced lines is to give you news of me and also to ask news of you. How have you been? Well, I'm sure. Here everything is in peace praise God. Your father took poison Nelo my son, this was the greatest sadness of my have pity on your mother I never asked you this it's the first time come get me you are the only person in this world do this for your poor old mother I beg you—

I draw close. I try to calm her.

"Mama, you're wrong. It wasn't Papa."

She pushes me. She punches at me, with a closed fist like a man, and hits me in the forehead. I draw away, rubbing my sore skin.

Nelo my son I have twelve children it's as if I didn't have any thank God I have you thank God—

She is quiet.

I imagine she must be very tired.

There is no more noise coming from the kitchen. The

coffin must be ready. Come here to the living room, come. There's another job for you, come. She is more yours than mine, come.

He clears his throat.

"There's somebody calling outside. Go see who it is."

"It's nobody. It's just the crazy man on the sidewalk outside the church."

The noise begins again. He's hammering. Before long he'll miss a nail and hit his finger. I don't dare to go in there. I have a horror of coffins. I can't sleep for days and days when I see one. It's even worse when the coffin is finished. The black cloth, that's what scares me most. Why black cloth? I just bought it a little while ago, in the store, on credit. I dragged it through the street, as if it were a white sheet. People drew back as I went by. Everyone is scared of black cloth, that's my consolation.

He doesn't know yet. He doesn't know that she (the boss-woman, your mother) is going to have to go on a long trip, from which she will probably never return. I will be her escort of honor. What else can I do?

"My son Nelo sent word—"

"When will he come and see his relatives, *compadre?*"

"One of these days when we're least expecting him."

"Here it is, *compadre,* the money you asked me for."

"Thank you very much. I'll pay it back right away, as soon as I can."

"It's in good hands, *compadre.* When you write to Nelo, remember me to him."

He is not afraid. He is capable of making a coffin, nailing the black lining in place, and even sleeping inside it a whole night. "What belongs to men the animals won't eat," he will think, no doubt, before falling asleep. How many coffins has he made? How many times has he rubbed his hands together, after the work was over, pleased at having done a good job? Saint Joseph was a carpenter, God is a carpenter. He is one of those people on familiar terms with death, calling it by little nicknames. But he will go to his own grave saying, "If there's one thing in this world I can't get used to..."

Come on, look at yourself. You are in front of the mirror, look at yourself.

He doesn't know it yet, but he soon will: it's he who will have to pay for everything. From the boards to the hole in the cemetery.

I hear him snore as he sits on the floor with his head leaning over on one shoulder. It's time I got things seen to, me of all people, so out of touch. I'll need to talk to the Mayor. My family—well, he'll have to take us. Farther into the night, farther, farther into the night.

Papa coughs. He works and coughs. He's smoking too much. He smokes and drinks too much.

Say: Give me your blessing, Mama. Say: God go with you.

"Her. Her. Her."

"Who, Papa?"


# VI

"Who made the shroud?"

"We don't have a shroud."

"Merciful heavens. Dear Lord, have mercy."

*Ora pro nobis.*

"To this day not one of our relatives has been buried

like that.''

"Well, then, this is the first."

"Mercif-"

"It so happens that none of the women, the aunts or cousins, turned up to make the shroud."

"And your mother, isn't she here? To let a son of hers be—"

My mother. Oh, my mother. Forget about her.

"I would have come over, but—"

Aunts and uncles. Cousins. Relatives.

They want to know what material is to be used for the shroud, just as before, when they wanted to know if my sheets were white or patterned. They came in and went straight to the bedrooms, then they took a look in the kitchen, fiddled with the pots and pans. Goggling. Gossiping. When you think they've all died or gone away, that's when they reappear. Trailing weeds? Were they what Nelo was talking about? Your name, please. The Trailing Weed family.

"Have you opened his suitcase?"

"Yes."

"And what had he brought?"

"Nothing."

"It's not possible. I don't believe it."

"You can go and look."

"I'd meant to go round, but—"

*The strangling vegetation that springs up with the rain and has to be pulled out.*

Pull everything out. Cornerpost, cornerpost, take your rotten tooth, give me mine back sound. Pull it out. Pain, sin, madness, early death. To be born again. In a house without bread, no one sees reason, and no one is fed.

Reason. Papa: people's reason is thin as a thread. One good shock is enough to—

To end the screams coming from the prison, to banish my fear of going there and taking the club away from the sergeant.

"Talk louder, Alcino," he shouted from the window. "Talk louder, Alcino, to cover the yelling." The crazy man howls from the door of the church while another man gets beaten inside the jail. We pretend we don't know. The cudgel weighs over two pounds. You can count the blows, from wherever you happen to be, in spite of crazy Alcino's sermon. Silent night. Correspondence courses in English, Universal Schools. I have already counted half a dozen blows on each hand. Listen: a child is getting a thrashing. He disobeyed his father, this child who is himself the father of ten children. He stole a chicken. He's a black man. "Bad people," says my aunt. "Shameless nigger. Maybe he'll mend his ways after this."

Tiago, the black man. Only yesterday he called me brother. Just because I bought him a drink.

"You're a lucky guy. You learned how to read and write. You got yourself a job that—"

He showed me his hands before picking up the billiard cue.

I bought him another drink and ordered one for myself. Around here we start early. As long as you're wearing long pants, nobody asks your age.

His hands: three enormous blisters on each one. He says they are callouses. Early in the morning he would be back at his hoe.

Hoe handle, rake handle, pickaxe, shovel. Three blisters on each hand.

"It's not every day there's work to do. I was lucky to find this."

I counted to ten, I couldn't count any further. Ten blows. Today the blisters will break. Ten kids. Tomorrow is another day at the hoe.

I was going to ask the Mayor for clemency before asking for the car. Alagoinhas. Fifteen leagues going, fifteen coming back. Some say it's fourteen, others say sixteen. On the way I meet the sergeant. There, the job is done. He sweats like a pig that has spent the day going round and round its pen. He had to use up a lot of energy. How many blows was it this time?

The average is a dozen on each hand.

"If I lay eyes on you once more today—"

A .38 caliber sergeant, long barrel. In the head? In the chest? In the belly? From behind? First let me take my mother to a—a home where—

The daughter of the deceased—the wife of—the mother of—

If everybody has his cross to bear, yours is—

People's reason is—

The Mayor is talking to himself, wandering around near the church. Not him, too? Now how will I manage? I can drive the car myself. But what about her? Who will hang onto her during the trip? There's still the driver who works for the Mayor. Is he asleep? No, nobody's asleep.

Screams come from the general store, other screams.

"No, Nelo! For the love of God, No! Forgive me, Nelo. I didn't mean it. A kid's trick. I'll order a Mass said for you. Not this, Nelo! Leave me alone. For your mother's sake. For my father's soul. For the love of Our Lord God."

Go ahead and yell, Pedro. Yes, cry, Pedro; kick,

scream, lose your mind. For the sake of us all, Pedro Infante.

The Mayor:

Tomorrow I'll get rid of that sergeant. Tomorrow I'm going to pave the square. I'll cut down those tamarind trees and build a park in the middle. Tomorrow, tomorrow. I'll get some motors to pump water. They didn't strike oil, they struck water. Mineral springs just like the ones on Itaparica Island, the men said; we'll pump that water. All with my own money, the state government doesn't give us a thing. Ser-geant? Every man to his post. Ser-geant? We need reinforcements. Ser-geant? Send for soldiers from Alagoinhas. If they don't want to send any, go to Salvador. Ser-geant? The king of France sent a message saying they want to depose me. My enemies are plotting in the silence of the night. Ser-geant? Quick, quick, hurry quick. The rebellion will break out tonight. Ser-geant? that man's a piece of shit.

"And they try to tell me that men have walked on the moon," said a countryman.

"Lot of talk," said one from the town.

"Sure a lot of crazy folks around."

"The day people start wanting to be greater than God, the end isn't far off."

The man from the country smiled, satisfied. He was in complete agreement.

Papa smiled too. The coffin was ready.

When he was a boy my son Nelo used to say: the earth is round like an orange. What I want to do is turn it.

And I said: nobody can say that. Nobody knows what the world is like.

My son Nelo used to say:

110

A man needs to be smart.

And I would say, "Well, now. Aren't we all smart enough? I'm smart."

He said, you need to be smart to stay alive.

He said:

The world is an oxcart that goes rolling forward, groaning on its axle.

I said, the world doesn't have an axle. It's held steady by the hands of God.

He said: the earth turns.

I said: if the earth turned, we'd all fall off.

He said: the earth turns very fast, that's why we don't fall off.

I said: if the earth turned, we would all get dizzy.

I thought: the earth turns like Mama's hand turning the wooden spoon to make soap inside the dish. Caustic soda and water. Soap serves to wash clothes. What do you use to wash the soul?

"If a snake bites you, put kitchen salt on the bite," the druggist explained to me. "As soon as the dizziness passes, drink some rum mixed with iodine."

"Is that all?"

"That's all. But I don't prepare medicines any more."

"Why not?"

"Because I don't have a diploma."

"And if the snake bites my reason?"

Papa, she's cra—cra—cra—

We have to go to a—in Alagoinhas. That's the closest one. Do you hear me? She has lost her—. Once and for all. He understood what I meant.

Then he said, Probably it's because the earth turns that there are so many crazy people.

Who, Papa? Who told you that?

"Jesus Christ, you son of a donkey."


# VII

A preview of Judgement Day. At least that's what it looked like to me. The square was full, like on a market day or the day of a holy pilgrimage. I was asking myself where so many people had come from, and why. The Mayor asked that measures be taken before the cock crowed thrice.

"Ser-geant!"

It was painful to see him that way; he really wasn't such a bad fellow.

"They want to depose me! They'll tar and feather me! I resist! Subversion! Rebellion!"

The sergeant ran off, some say to hide under his bed. And I didn't have time to reassure the Mayor that nothing was happening. It was only a collection of men and women wandering about through the town, silent, as if they didn't know each other, as if not one of them had anything to do with any of the others. The Mayor continued to shout.

"They're all armed, but I won't surrender! I resist. The Antichrist can't take my power from me—I resist. Sergeant!"

But the words that accompanied me along the road were those of mad Alcino:

*With my rags I'll cover you,*
*And you will be protected.*
*Come, and I will shelter you.*
*You won't feel heat or cold,*
*Pain or fear.*

112

*Come, and I will shelter you.*
*Seven palmspans has your bed,*
*You'll sleep so soundly.*
*Come, and I will shelter you.*
*The rain drops on the flowers,*
*Soft is your coverlet.*
*Come, and I will shelter you.*
*I am the road, I am the end of the road.*
*Come—*

# PART FOUR

## The Land Takes Me Back

"WE'RE GOING for a little ride." An answer can be entirely true, partly true, or can mean absolutely nothing. Would you be able to lie to your own mother?

"Are we going for a ride? Where are we going?"

Questions. An entire lifetime of questions. Where were you, out until this hour? Who were you with? What were you doing? No half-baked explanations, or the whip will sing on your backside.

Any answer at all will be a lie. She never had an apron all dirty with egg; she never had an apron. Country people: what we were, what we are, what we always will be. But she had a slipper in her hand, I remember. Promise you'll sleep the whole trip, do you promise? Then we'll get there faster. Say your prayers if you want, it will make you sleepy. The seat is soft, you can have a nice nap there. Lean your head back. Sleep, sleep. Rest. It will be only a few hours. We are going for a ride, yes, we're going for a ride. We'll be swept along by the tide at forty miles an hour on account of the holes in the road. Then it gets better; pretty soon we'll come to the asphalt. It's straight ahead, as far as Inhambupe.

The floods washed away the fences, and now they're taking my mother, through the dark night. Where do these waters flow? To the Inhambupe River. Where does the

Inhambupe River go? To the sea. My mother will turn into a mermaid. I always thought she had a mermaid's body.

"Why didn't you get a better horse? This one's bumpy, his paces are hard as the devil. By the time we get there I'll be saddle-sore. I'm already getting dizzy."

She vomits onto my legs. Dizzy. She used to have this nausea every year, a little before her belly began to swell. Children, one a year and each one was a new horror. Papa used to say "Sickening woman!" Was that why? I roll down the window and push her face outside. The wind blows strings of her vomit onto my clothes, into my face, everywhere. The trees are going by quickly, like silver smudges. I hope the time will pass quickly.

"Too bad I didn't place a bet today. I think my number would have come up."

Nelo, brother, she wastes all the money you send on the lottery, in strange wagers and installments that never end. I thought that after she paid for the television she would settle down, but she didn't. When the money is late coming, she starts tearing out her hair, unable to cope with so many creditors at the door. The old man has to sweat to provide for everybody, poor thing, and he lives from hand to mouth, doing an odd job here and there when he can. She still complains. She spends her life complaining and saying that he doesn't support them. Then the fighting starts. Battles rage. The money you send evaporates, nobody even sees the color of it. Excommunicated. I feel sorry for the kids. They go hungry, Nelo. You should see how miserable life is in that house. Papa complains about his bad luck. He says the move to Feira de Santana was the worst misfortune of his life. He never understood anything. He never will.

"You know what it is for a man to lose control of things?" I've heard your complaints, old man, contrary to what you think, and I believe you're right. Everybody's right. It's the world that is wrong.

It's not the earth that is spinning, it's my head, as if I were falling about, drunk. Fatigue, worry, insomnia and the bumping of the rattle-trap car with three people inside: her, myself and the Mayor's driver, who came along with a bad grace. Well, it's very late, poor guy. At least he came. I have to put up with all this and tend to the new arrivals, that is, those who might show up for the funeral. My land doesn't have palm trees like it says in the poem; it has the juice of strangling weeds. Sap, they say around here. Top-quality poison. Have you ever smelled your own mother's vomit?

"I have to do everything all by myself," she complains. "Nobody helps me. Not one of my daughters is willing to wash my dirty clothes and give me some clean ones to put on. Have the boys already gone to school?"

I do what I should have done some time ago, support her back and rearrange her gently so she gains a better position at the car window. She goes back to cursing her lot. "What a headache. I feel my head is going to explode. Are you taking me to a doctor? I feel so terrible."

To be torn apart with pain as though in a flood: pain from the liver, the intestines, the kidneys, the heart. She was going blind too. Nobody realized that she was going blind. Already she couldn't thread a needle. "I left so much sewing to finish."

"I'm going to write to Nelo. He has to come here to take me to a doctor. Why is it that Nelo never comes?"

This time it's I who feel a great pain. In my soul? She

has seen his dead body and didn't believe it. You can't kill her golden dream, that must be it. "Before you woke me up, I had the most horrible nightmare. I dreamed he had died. It was horrible. Nelo's still so young. May God give him many years yet, that's all I ask."

"Friend, drive a little slower. She's not feeling too well," I say to the driver.

"That's the reason I'm going so fast. The sooner we arrive, the better, don't you think?"

"*Compadre* Ioiô? Are we in *Compadre* Ioiô's jeep?"

"No, Mama. We're in the Mayor's car."

"Oh, fine. That's better than an oxcart. You know something? I don't miss those trips we used to make in oxcarts. They used to take so long."

The horse-and-buggy era. And me stuck in the asshole of the world. An entire week hanging around the little streets of Inhambupe, where I didn't know a soul, and not a penny in my pocket. A whole week waiting for a truck to give me a lift, because the horse that had brought me ran away and went home all by itself. They say horses can find their way by the scent. Now people say "You see? Things have changed. Now you can leave São Paulo and get here on the same day." And it's true. We discovered the wheel and we're turning, nearly always with great imprudence: all you have to do is count the crosses at the roadside. Crosses, Cruzes. Aunts and uncles. Cousins. Relatives. Those who went to their final rest beneath the wheels. And I still ask myself: have things changed? What has really changed?

"It's been so long since I was here that I've forgotten what people look like. I so much wanted to see *Compadre* Ioiô."

"He's in Salvador. He went to see his daughter."

120

"Daughter! Don't talk to me about daughters."

Once she said to me, "I wish I had been born a man."

And, playfully, I asked her, "What for? So you could work with a hoe?"

Then she said something that to this day makes me think. "No, that's not why. Plenty of women use a hoe when they have to. I wish I was a man so I could control my own life. To go anywhere I liked, without having to give anybody the time of day."

Daughter. Don't talk to me about daughters.

"I really wish I had only sons."

We bounce about on the coils of springs. No longer does the earth turn like the axle of an oxcart; life is hurried. My mother leans her head against my shoulder, then moves away. She begins to writhe, her face contorting with the same expression it had when she was beating herself against the wall. It was the first time she had ever leaned her head against my shoulder. We're rough people; we don't know what affection is. They offer it to us when we are small, then later refuse it, maybe through lack of custom. Do you wear long trousers? Then you're a man. And if you're a man, all your gestures have to be rough. Brutality. Force. Character. Men's things, like the Holy Trinity.

She begins to tear at herself. She has unbelievable strength. She tears at herself with all the brutality that mothers offer their sons. I try to hold her hands down. It's difficult, but I am trying. The expression on her face fills me with terror. "Daughter. Don't talk to me about daughters." Now I fear the worst. She won't make it. I see the end in her face. What if she dies? It'll be back home for two funerals. It seems simple, but it isn't.

Damned by her own nature. Five daughters, five women, five times cursed. "A vulture shit on my luck," I can hear her utter, as I begin to pray, not just any prayer, but the verses that she said her oldest son (the beloved Nelo) used to recite out in the fields when he was a child, to everyone's amazement: Don't cry, my child, don't cry, /For life is a hard battle,/ Life is a struggle to the end.

"Nelo, my son, I have the scars. You never knew because I never let you find out." The shot had torn into the calf of her leg, gouging out a piece of flesh. She wasn't inventing it. The mark is still there.

Yes, yes, I think, tell me everything. You can't die without unloading that burden. It still hurts, doesn't it?

It wasn't just the memory of the shot. It was a whole drama. Five daughters, five dramas.

From the look of her, I'd say the hour has come. Have you ever seen death close up? Face to face? It's ugly. There is nothing uglier in this world. "Tell me, Mama. How was it?"

"Adelaide was in bed, resting. She had had a baby the day before. She was showing me the cut on her belly. She was crying. It was her husband who had done that. He was jealous, jealous of the doctor who delivered the baby, just imagine! I was horrified, and then he came in, shooting. One bullet got me in the leg. The others were all discharged into your sister's stomach."

"Then she didn't die in childbirth?"

"I just told you that to cover up. No, it wasn't childbirth."

The axles of her eyes must be damaged. They don't turn any more. They look like two upholstered buttons that have faded and lost their shine. What must they be seeing?

"What I suffered on account of those girls..."

Mama convinces me. That is the strangest thing: she always could convince me. Everyone is right. That is the truth: everyone is right.

"Poor dead Adelaide. My daughter. May God keep her in His hands. I warned her, 'Be careful of that man.' I don't understand a woman's nature. She didn't like him, was always avoiding him, until the minute I said that. What did I go and say it for? She ran off the very next day. I went through the very worst suffering of my life for the next three days. I looked for her everywhere: the police station, the hospital, hotels. You know where she was? In a brothel, locked in a room. She couldn't even talk to me. Locked in and getting beaten. I went back to the police station and told the officer everything. So he said he would do something about it, and he did. She got married at the police station, because she was under age. She spent the rest of her life getting beaten up, and the more he beat her, the wilder she seemed to be for that man."

How many times did we hear those old stories? You knew them by heart, Nelo. She had a lot of secrets put away for you, brother, at the bottom of the trunk. Now at last she's opened it up. See? Hear? Smell? It's all for you, wherever you are. And now she thinks I'm you.

The changes began with you, because you were the first to take to the road. But we only heard good news from you. Your star brightened our dark nights. There were callouses on our hands from grinding corn with the big mortar and pestle. As we worked we'd complain about our life, the girls most of all:

*Spend your life grinding corn*
*Spend your life hauling water.*

*Spend your life grating manioc,*
*Spend your life pulling beans.*

God heard the song, the sad old refrain, day and night. We learned that He was our cousin and lived in Feira de Santana. He called two of our sisters into His Kingdom. A Kingdom full of light—the light of learning, at a state school. With two sisters in this enchanted world, the rest of us began to redouble our prayers and sing our song louder than ever; for the dominions of God must be limitless, surely there was room for us all. There wasn't. We came to realize that there were limitations, laws, prohibitions all around us. Then the letters began to arrive: God was angry because the girls were chasing after boyfriends. He threatened to send them back, for He didn't like young girls who chased after boys. I can still see Mama with a letter in her hand, frowning and shaking her head, somewhere between desperation and resolve. She was very calm, or seemed to be, when she said,

"They're not coming back—I'll go there. And you'll come along afterwards." This was not to prove an easy decision, because of Papa, as usual.

There were anxious days ahead—confusion, quarreling, he-said-you-said. And many prayers. Not a single saint was left in peace, they were all called upon to intervene in our favor. Everybody wanted to go. Papa was all alone. The old lady pulled out her hair and stamped her foot. She was firm in her resolution: I never saw her so determined. She said:

"My father took me out of school for writing a note— the first and only time—to a boy in my class. I can't let the same thing happen to my daughters."

And she didn't, to do her justice. We all ended up

huddling into a poor little house in a shantytown with no electricity, water, drainage, or plumbing. Mama depended on the money you sent every month to pay the rent and when it was late coming, God help us. We lived in permanent fear of being put out in the street. She began to work as a seamstress, worked like thirty women at her sewing machine, while waiting for the beans and rice that the old man sent from the country. Once in a while he would turn up to complain about everything. I think Mama wore herself out with work partly out of personal pride, fear of failing, so Papa wouldn't be able to say "I told you so". Even so we continued to live in a house a thousand times worse than the one we had lived in in the country. Our consolation was that we could walk to high school, that is, we could go to high school.

"After the first one ran away, all the others wanted to follow in her footsteps." She kept speaking jerkily, like the gears changing in this car. Again I tell the driver to take it easy. He can't wait to get there. We're already onto the paved highway. The worst twenty-five miles are over. Sometimes I think it's these twenty-five miles that make all the difference. "It still pains my memory, Nelo my son, it still hurts. You don't know what it is for a mother to have to spend her life running up and down like a lunatic trying to find her daughters, and never knowing whether they'll turn up dead or alive. You don't know what it is to be ashamed, because you're not a woman and you don't know." The tears run down her old, lined face. The ravages of time. "Be patient, Mama, we must be patient." There's a point after which words are useless, I know, but I need to talk to you. The evil hour. What can I do to calm her? These could be her last moments, there's no point in rushing any more. Father, husband, children: the rotten teeth of time. With your body you will satisfy the earth's hunger. What can I do so you will have an easy death? "The shame of having to walk up and down after a doctor to get him to say whether the baby my girl was carrying belonged to the man who'd taken her away."

"But that one's doing all right, isn't she?"

"She's alive. And even well treated."

"So let's forget the past. It's better to leave it all behind."

"Certain things we never forget. I'll never forget."

I remember, of course I remember.

The place was called Maragogipe and it was a hell of a distance away. We would never find her, because we would never know where to look in such an unfamiliar area. Once all the trails had been searched, combed, and investigated, we stopped to rest. The case was hopeless. "Did a girl pass this way about this height, this sort of hair...? Her name is Noemia, Noemia Lopes Cruz." Mama wore out her feet. One day she walked twelve miles on the road to Irará. Why did she take the road to Irará? Because when you don't know which way to go, any direction will do. All the exit routes had to be examined, hill by hill, clod by clod. It was about then that she started hitting Papa on the occasions he came to see us to grumble. And not a clue in hell as to what road Noemia had taken. Maragogipe. Six months later a man came to us with some news. He hadn't come to console us, to put an end to so much worrying and suffering. The girl he had taken away with him was pregnant, and now he was informing us that he was going to give her back to her parents. It seemed he had made a mistake. He had taken a girl who was no virgin, and he couldn't live with a woman who had soiled herself with another man before him. He couldn't even be sure if there had been only one or several. Therefore he didn't feel responsible for what was inside her belly, which was already starting to show. Mama was patiently pressing a pair of trousers on the tabletop. She heard him out without saying a single word. When the man was done talking, she got up and poked her finger at his face. He was a fairly young man, on the short side, with light-brown skin and straight hair evenly cut. He seemed a decided person, the sort who wouldn't let an insult pass by unchallenged. But now he was looking very yellow, his face tense and fearful, as if he had forgotten what he had come to do.

"You're a son of a bitch!" was what Mama was telling him, her ferocious finger advancing ever closer to his face. Shrinking back into his chair, the man shook his head, as if to defend himself from a mortal blow. "What's more, I hope I live to put a bullet into your filthy mouth!" Defeated by the unexpected violence of a woman who told him, "Your mother wasn't even human, you were whelped by a cow!" and who seemed to grow, to acquire monstrous forms before his eyes, the man (reduced now to the size of a mouse) whirled about in his chair and made as if to run away in his alarm and confusion. Unluckily for him, I had locked the door. "Wait a minute," I said. "Let's decide how we're going to settle all this."

He had fallen into a trap and was brought to bay. That was when he spoke of a doctor. He wanted to hear an unbiased opinion as to the blood-type of the baby my sister was carrying. If it was proven that the baby was not somebody else's, then he would stay with my sister. He

127

would even marry her, although only in the church way (which was, actually, the solution to everything—for our people, the religious ceremony is what counts; the civil wedding means nothing). That's the least of my troubles, said the old lady with regard to procuring a doctor. And off she went in the direction of Maragogipe, accompanying the man on a long, silent journey. I asked myself how many curses, how many insults, how many horrors must be sticking in her throat. She came back the next day, escorted by a whole battalion: her daughter, her daughter's husband, the husband's parents and even a brother of the husband. It was never known just what Noemia had said to the doctor in private, only that, after speaking to her privately, he had ordered the blood test. Everything came out fine. So fine that she now has eight children and all of them, they say, are the spitting image of their father.

"All they ever brought me was trouble." Her voice is dragging, mournful. It makes one think of time passing, of that hour when the day is dying on the red edges of the horizon and people recite the Hail-Mary. That's what our lives have been like—a constant sunset. "I was getting ready for bed when I heard a funny noise, the noise of somebody jumping out of a window. I thought it was a thief. I went to look into the girl's room—they should have been asleep a long time ago. I still had three daughters left, that was what I was thinking. When I went into the room, I saw Zuleide kneeling on her bed, closing the window. I asked her what was going on. She answered, 'Just what you're thinking.' The other girls were asleep, or pretending to be, in their bunk beds. Zuleide got off her bed and stood up in the middle of the room. She said again: 'Exactly what you're thinking, Mama. If you want to kill me, go

128

ahead. But it's the truth.' The other two knew all about it, because they saw it all, every night. They hadn't said anything to me. That's what I never understood: why didn't they tell me?''

The night wind is cold blowing through the car window. We need a lot of air in here. She has already vomited up everything that was inside her; the problem now is the smell. "Faster," I ask the driver this time. We have to get her there alive. I can't keep my eyes very wide open because of the wind. It blows my hair backward, it blows me backward, it throws me into the sweeping current of time.

"So I sent a message to your father: 'Come and get this girl. She can't stay here with me. You take care of her from now on. Put her to work with a hoe.' When she found out her father was really coming, you know what Zuleide did?''

"Hey Dina, wait. Zilda, come over here."

The three were coming home from school. They formed a little group, distant from the other students.

"Are you two going straight home?" asked Zuleide.

"Yes, why?"

"Well, say good-bye to everyone for me. A big good-bye."

"Aren't you coming?"

"Look over there." Zuleide pointed to a tree. "See that taxi?"

"Yes, what about it?"

"Nothing. Tell Papa that the country is for the birds." She ran off, leaping like a child playing hopscotch, while the other two girls stared at each other without a word. Every so often Zuleide would stop, look back and wave to them.

"Aren't you going to even leave us an address?" one of them shouted.

"I'll write to you," said Zuleide, running again.

She wrote a year later from a place called Pojuca, saying she had just had a little girl. She would be happy to welcome visitors. Her door was always open to everyone. Later, when the baby was bigger, she would take her to meet the relatives. It was a very funny letter which ended like this: "Tell Papa that the country is for the birds." My sisters would have remembered this and had a good laugh. Pity the letter never reached them: they too were already gone. Long gone.

The droning of the car motor is as persistent as the anxiety inside me. Hurry, Totonhim, hurry to save your mother, so that you may save yourself: it's your only hope. Medicine, drugs, magic spells, prayers, whatever-the-hell crosses your mind. As the car tears down the road you could imagine the highway piercing the heart, the navel, the arsehole of Brazil. Salvador, Bahia for the Baianos. Recife-Pernambuco speaking to the world. Hello, hello, testing, loudspeaker testing. This is the Voice of the Backlands with another musical offering, this time for the girl in blue and white who at this very minute is strolling down the street beside the church, arm in arm with the girl in pink and yellow. Colors and flowers go crazy too. Satan pleads for mercy, it's too dry in hell. Salvador, the capital of love. May I have your attention, please! God will speak today over the national TV network, attention Junco, turn on your twenty-odd sets tonight at eight o'clock. God is going to speak. He exists. What He doesn't want is to get involved. My mother ought to hear this. My mother ought to know: God is the biggest son-of-a-bitch in the history of mankind.

"No, my son, you're wrong. I am only addressing those who exploit My Holy Name. I assure you they don't do so in vain."

"And the money we give to the priest, in Thy Holy Name?"

"That's the priest's problem, plus whoever invented the custom."

"You mean you do hear me, sir, uh, Your Excellency—hell, how is it people should address you?"

"Each person has his own manner. But I'd prefer you not to swear."

"So you do exist?"

"I clothe myself with the sun and the moon, I adorn myself with stars and wear a lightning shaft on each arm. Do you want to know the truth? I'm the national champion of all fancy-dress competitions, like Carnival, that's why they say I am Brazilian."

She leans her head on my shoulder for the second and last time in her life. She is exhausted.

"Mama, Mama, I spoke with Him. Now I know everything."

"Be quiet," she says. "I'm so tired."

She falls asleep.

Dawn is breaking: it must be between four and five o'clock. I can ask the time when we reach the big town: the businessmen who came from far and wide to settle there hold perfect dominion over its hours. We're nearly there. Alagoinhas is a world of doors that open and close, a life in two tenses, open and shut, shut and open, only two movements in time. Filthy hotels and boarding houses for the country boys who come to study here, for truck drivers who pass through. Four or five schools, doors that open and shut. The whorehouse is on the righthand side as you enter town, the hospital on the left. I still don't know if I should take her to the hospital, the asylum, or the funeral parlor. Have you ever heard the convulsive snoring of your own mother? I have a whole lot of relatives living in shacks and shanties here on the outskirts of the town; they took over a whole neighborhood. They'll be waking up now—as if they were still on the farm. They wallow in the ghetto, in the sewers. You don't have to go far to see: they're right here in Alagoinhas, Bahia. Miserable life of misery, I can't bear to think of another two hundred years of drought, another century of hunger. Peasants form lines at the doors of other peasants now living in the city. The neighborhood on the outskirts of town is the smelliest, the most wretched of all. This place is just like Feira de Santana. I know, I used to live there.

Your thought is the product of your own madness, the doorman of the asylum seems to say. He's sleepy, drab and mean-looking. A world of sad people, all looking like me. You're right, confirms the nurse with a dried-up little face, her eyes hidden behind glasses. Wilted, like the vegetables for sale on the stand outside. A nervous type, like my mother. "The director is still asleep," she informs me. "Why?" I ask her.

She looks at me over her glasses, and the answer is in her tired eyes: because you're too early. I think: no, we're too late. She lowers her eyes, and I can almost hear her say,

"You know what it's like to work night shift in a madhouse, then be waked up by a man and woman smelling like you?"

We'll wait. The director doesn't arrive until eight o'clock, so I pace back and forth countless times from one end of the sidewalk to the other. The driver is leaning over the steering wheel, fast asleep; Mama is sleeping, curled up on the back seat of the car. Children pass happily on their way to school, girls wearing navy and white, boys wearing khaki uniforms. Bury your dead, children; the future is blue and white. Or, as Papa used to say, the future belongs to God.

Fortunately, the director turns out to be Jonga, who became a friend during the last election, when he was in Junco drumming up votes for a cousin of his. I even found him a few. He sent me a letter afterwards, thanking me and placing himself at my disposal. I wasn't ashamed to present myself just as I was, looking like hell, or to introduce my mother under the circumstances. Two ragpickers. It's painful to say it, but true. Jonga was very cordial, sympathetic even. He tried to console me.

"If we all have a cross to bear, you've certainly borne yours."

Mama would receive the best possible treatment, I could trust him and put my mind at rest. As we were talking she said,

"What a handsome doctor! Haven't I seen him on television?"

I've thought about this thing called solidarity between people. It does exist, as long as we know somebody who is in a position to offer it. At least around here it's been that way. It's more like an exchange of favors.

They didn't wait for me to go ahead with the funeral. Just as well. Tired as I was, I only wanted to fall into a bed and close my eyes. Papa moaned:

133

"There were hardly any people."

"So what are you going to do now, Papa?"

"I'm going on a little trip through the country, to visit some of the relatives. Tomorrow I'll take the bus to Alagoinhas, and from there I'll go to Feira."

Travel around and visit the relatives—that was what he most enjoyed.

"It's going to cost money, don't you know? Every month."

"I'm pretty hard up. One week there's work, one week there isn't."

"And what I earn is very little."

"Every bit helps."

"Papa, I don't think you understand me. Mama...what do you plan to do?"

"See if I can find one of these girls in the family to come and take care of the house."

An old man and three kids. Four helpless people.

"And Mama? The asylum, money every month."

"I won't last much longer. I feel sure of that."

It was then that I too began to feel lost, helpless, alone. All that remained was a monstrous absurdity—absurd Mother, absurd Father, absurd Me. "Your life hangs by a thread of pure chance." And you are the child of that chance. The revulsion comes as before, only greater now, more dangerous. You will not die from shock, a stray bullet or sinful living, Totonhim. You will sink in a swamp of problems, the sweet inheritance they have left you. The funeral was paid for with borrowed money. Wretchedness comes from wretchedness born of wretchedness. Your father doesn't know if he'll have enough to eat from now on, let alone if he'll be able to pay off his son's funeral. He's telling you that he spent his life working hard, nobody could ever call him lazy, and all that's left to him are two hands covered with callouses. And when you ask him the third time, "What do you plan to do, Papa?" he answers, "If I weren't so old, I'd go to São Paulo or Paraná." Maybe he was wanting me to push him down the road. Dear Nelo, I'm not going to cry over your death. You went at the right time. Now I'm beginning to understand you, indeed I am.

"You know something, Papa—I'm going away."

"Where to?"

"The money I get from the Mayor's office at the end of the month will buy my ticket."

He insisted: "Where to?"

"It's not much, but I think it'll be enough to get me there."

"You've got your job here. For better or worse, you've got something steady here. Take your time."

"You may not know, but I have a cow out in grandpa's field, may he rest in peace. If I sell her, I'll have enough."

"But where are you going?"

"To São Paulo."

If there is one thing I don't understand, it's this: why the old man could never accept an idea from one of us. We had to present the thing already done, for him even to consider it—against his will.

"You're just like the others. You don't like it here." He spoke in a harsh tone, as if he had jumped backward in time and suddenly become the father of former days. "Nobody likes it here. Nobody has any love for this land."

He did—I knew, everyone knew.

The sermon over, Papa's voice softened. He seemed

more accepting, less displeased.

"You're doing the right thing," he said. "Follow the example—"

He lowered his eyes, without finishing what he was going to say.

ABOUT THE TRANSLATOR: Margaret A. Neves is a North American living in Brazil, where she specializes in translating contemporary Brazilian authors like Moacyr Scliar (*The Centaur in the Garden*) and Antônio Torres.